THE POTUS PAPERS
By
Bryan Mooney

Books by Bryan Mooney

The Potus Papers
Love Letters
A Second Chance

Dedication

This novel is dedicated to Bonnie, my wonderful, loving wife. Thank you.

Acknowledgements

I would like to thank all of those individuals, who helped me along the way to the final completion of this novel including my "special advisors & readers," which include Cindy & Ray Goetzinger, Judy Hanses, Danielle Goetzinger, Carol Kayne, Michael Naver and especially my loving wife Bonnie, my toughest critic. Their guiding hands and direction kept this ship on its proper chosen course and their insights, patience and encouragement throughout the process were invaluable.

Also, this novel would not be possible without the incredible talents of my extremely versatile editor, Eliza Knight.

I can't thank all of you enough. Thank you. - BDM

.

Introduction

Nick Ryan is one of the FBI's top investigators before he takes a temporary leave to track down his wife's killer. A former agency friend hires him to verify a simple suicide claim for his insurance company. Nick sees it as an open and shut case, until he meets the victim's beautiful daughter, Adriana. She convinces him that her father would never commit suicide and asks him to investigate further. Nick soon discovers that everyone her father had talked to prior to his death is turning up dead.

The headstrong investigator pursues every lead across three continents, until the trail ends with the President of the United States, POTUS as he is called by the Secret Service. No one is who they appear to be. Suddenly, Nick Ryan finds he is next on the list to die. Nick is running out of time. He must solve the mystery of, The POTUS Papers…

Chapter One

The Arabic message he texted was short and to the point. Yasim did not like texting about such sensitive matters but time was of the essence. He had to let his father know quickly.

FATHER-

THE VIRUS IS LOOSE!

KITMAN MAY BE IN JEOPARDY.

URGENTLY NEED GLOBAL SPECIALISTS TO CONTAIN AND INOCULATE.

THREE HAVE BEEN INFECTED BUT HAVE ALREADY BEEN INOCULATED.

WILL PREPARE AN INOCULATION LIST.

WILL SANITIZE HERE

I AWAIT YOUR RESPONSE.

YASIM

He looked down at the lifeless body lying at his feet in the center of the room. Blood pooled from the head, seeping into the rug.

Yasim searched the entire apartment again and once more found nothing. He was desperate. The more people that came in contact with what he was looking for, meant more people would die. He did not care how many people died but the damage it could do to the Kingdom, to their world and more importantly to his father's project, would be irreparable. It was imperative that he find it before it was too late.

He was going to need help, lots of help, but for now he must keep searching. That was his job, the reason his father dispatched him to Baltimore from the embassy in DC.

The dead man, Joseph Santino provided no clues. Yasim scoured the hallway before leaving apartment number 802 and hurried past number 805, the former apartment of Hakim Maheed the neighbor and close friend of Joseph Santino. Yellow and black police tape still flapped from the wall across the apartment entry door. Lifting the lifeless tape, he opened the door to Maheed's apartment for one last search. He had to find what he'd been sent to retrieve or find some clues as to where it was. He knew his father was depending on him.

• • •

The message had its predictable responses and some unanticipated consequences as it hit the airwaves on its way to Yasim's father, Prince Rashid, in Jeddah, Saudi Arabia.

"Jarem," Prince Rashid called out to his most trusted bodyguard, "get me a secure line. My son may wish to share this information with the Americans at the NSA, but I do not wish to give them anymore than what they may already have. I am sure they have this information already, thanks to my son. And if they have this information, I guarantee you that the Israelis have it as well."

He shook his head in anguish. "How many times have I told my son not to use text to communicate such sensitive information as this? He tries to code information thinking he will fool people. The Americans are not stupid, brash and vulgar yes, but stupid, no. And this information of all things, the most sensitive information to our cause. What am I going to do with him?"

"He is young," responded Jarem, "he will learn our ways, I am sure of it." Jarem liked the Prince's youngest son and always stood up for him whenever his father spoke ill of him.

"In battles you have only one chance to defeat your enemy, to be a man, if not you perish. He has worked in our Washington Embassy for too long. My son has been softened by Western ways and has grown accustomed to them. I will need to handle it."

Jarem started to respond and the Prince raised his hand to silence him. "I know, Jarem, you love him as do I, but he must learn." The Prince waved his hand for privacy, and Jarem left the palatial suite.

Taking a deep breath, Rashid smelled the scent of the sweet desert flowers wafting through his high palace windows. They reminded him of his youth and the times that he spent in the desert sands with his own father. He remembered the hunts, the raids, the battles and the wild victory celebrations that followed. But today was no day to celebrate; today was a day to make decisions.

He placed his phone calls and set his plan into motion. It must be stopped and stopped now. They had come too far. They must not be defeated.

Chapter Two

Returning from lunch, Luke Garrison showed his National Security Agency badge to the first of three security guards at the NSA Fort Meade Headquarters. They always surveyed his ID photo longer than anyone else's badge. The picture on his badge showed him with shorter hair and clean shaven. Now he had long, curly locks of blond beachcomber hair and a full reddish, black beard. He was a sight to behold for these security officials, who had no sense of humor whatsoever.

After running his corned beef and rye sandwich, mp3 player and backpack through the ultraviolet scanner, he was ready to return to his subterranean office to finish his work and hopefully get a jump on the weekend. Today he would like to get out of work at a decent hour, see his fiancé and spend some time with her.

He pressed the elevator key thumbprint pad and inserted his badge into the security slot, then boarded the express elevator for a quick ride. The elevator felt as if it hardly moved, when in fact it had traveled the thirteen floors underground in record time.

Jerry West was at his desk poring through a pile of intercepts. "Did you bring me my Ham N' Swiss on Rye?" he asked of his co-worker. "Jesus Luke, don't tell me you forgot again. You forgot my sandwich. Well, you are just going to have to sit here and cover for me while I run out and get my own lunch. Thanks a lot. I'll remember this the next time you want something from Epstein's Deli."

Luke Garrison left his jacket on his chair because he did not need it outside on the unusually warm May afternoon in suburban Maryland. But inside the cavernous computer room was another story. Luke swore that he had seen it snow at times when the machines were running at top speed and the air-conditioning rose to the challenge to keep the computers cool.

Deep in the heart of the building in suburban Maryland just outside of Baltimore, Luke wondered what he was doing here. He had never anticipated that he would use his Computer Science degree from Cal Tech, sitting in a huge computer warehouse poring over suspect telephone and text messages from around the globe.

Any moron could do this, he thought disgustedly. In his six years here, nothing exciting had ever happened, other than the time a mouse got into the computer room. The rodent drove everyone crazy setting off the motion detectors until they caught it, luckily before it did any damage to the delicate equipment.

He leaned back in his chair, popped open his soda and unwrapped his sandwich. He was alone in this huge room other than the multi-billion dollar pieces of hardware to keep him company.

What another day of drudge, he thought as he tasted the same old corned beef and rye that he'd been ordering since Christmas. After the Fourth of July he would change to ordering something different, maybe he would go with Ham 'n Swiss but skip the mayo. But he had two months to think about it before making up his mind. Suddenly the chatter box display screen began to hum and the control panel lit up with all of the computers talking to each other in their rapid response format.

"What's going on?" he said out loud to no one in particular. He tossed his unfinished sandwich into the trash. The machines increased their tempo. The red lights flashed on his control board. He spun his chair around and moved under his keyboard to take command. This is what he had been trained for and this was when the rubber met the proverbial road. He was ready.

The machines continued at a fever pitch, before beginning to collate and then assimilate the information and produce an intelligence report. This process used to take two to three weeks when he first came here six years ago but now it was done in a matter of seconds. He retrieved the sheet from the high speed printer and read the message:

Classified Agency Top Secret

Director - Eyes Only—Level Six

FATHER—

THE VIRUS IS LOOSE!

KITMAN MAY BE IN JEOPARDY.

URGENTLY NEED GLOBAL SPECIALISTS TO CONTAIN AND INOCULATE.

THREE HAVE BEEN INFECTED BUT HAVE ALREADY BEEN INOCULATED.

WILL PREPARE AN INOCULATION LIST.

WILL SANITIZE HERE

I AWAIT YOUR RESPONSE.

YASIM

Process Immediately according to Protocol Level Six.

Message sent from CONUS (Continental United States) TO KOSA (Kingdom Of Saudi Arabia) — Unscrambled message from Crown Prince Yasim in Suburban Maryland to his father, Saudi Prince Rashid, Jeddah Saudi Arabia. Of note, origination point is same building as residence of the late Hakim Maheed.

Message transcribed from Yasim at 13:52 Zulu time — via Motorola text phone model #2034A, non-secured communications tool. — End

Wow, what a hot potato! Luke wished he had gotten Jerry his sandwich because he could really use his help and input. After a few moments of deliberation he finally picked up his phone and followed protocol, calling the Intelligence Director, Jack Drury a Staff Naval Commander.

"Commander Drury please, Analyst Garrison calling with a Level Six message." This was the highest level message Luke had ever seen. He had seen level twos before, but never a level six. Protocol required that all Level Six Communiqués have an immediate response to the highest levels, rather than in the Blue Book which was collected at the end of the day.

"Bring that to me now," was the immediate response when Drury's aide, Colonel Parker Johnston picked up the phone. "Mark it Level Six, ROTC—Reporting of Terrorist Communications—Directors Eyes Only. Bring it to me STAT."

Luke grabbed his tie off the coat rack in the corner of the tiny office he shared with Jerry and sprinted towards the elevator, tying his tie in the process. After three attempts he finally completed the process as the door opened on the executive floor of the building. He was greeted at the elevator by Colonel Parker Johnston. Luke shook the big man's hand in silence and they started their long walk down the green carpeted hallway.

Drury and Johnston had been in the CIA together during the wild days of Intelligence gathering before being removed from the field and assigned a desk job at NSA headquarters. They had both crossed the line in using unauthorized interrogation techniques on prisoners to gather information to save the life of one of their field operatives who'd been kidnapped. They got the information one hour too late. Their associate was found dead two days later, beheaded.

Drury and Johnston were still in the doghouse with the bureaucrats because of the way they got the information. Now they were both looking for something that would redeem them and get them back in the field.

"Walk with me," commanded Johnston, while he reviewed the contents of the intercept. When he finished reading, he stopped walking and turned to Garrison asking, "Has anyone else seen this?"

"No sir, no one." Luke straightened his crooked tie.

"Keep it that way. Do not mention it to anyone. Do you understand? No one."

"Yes, sir."

"Okay, you are free to return to your office but remember, do not tell anyone of this document. Am I clear?"

"Yes sir, perfectly clear."

Commander Johnston turned and left the young computer scientist to find his way back down the long hallway, preparing to discuss the Intercept Report with his boss, Jack Drury.

He closed the door behind him, not really wanting to interrupt his long time friend today, not this day of all days. Today was the beginning of Drury's annual hearings in front of the closed Congressional Committee on Intelligence Funding; never a good day for Jack Drury.

But he had to bring him up to date. They talked for over fifteen minutes until NSA Director Drury finally asked his trusted aide, "PJ, what's your take on all of this?"

Johnston leaned back in the worn brown leather sofa and studied his friend. "The same as you, Jack, its not what it appears to be. Somebody has an overactive imagination but I detect the same undercurrent as you, and I don't like it one bit. We need to send this to the CIA and FBI, now."

"What about…?"

"Yeah, get your coat, we're going for a little ride to the White House. The President needs to see this. I'll have Mary call over and tell them we're on our way."

He pressed the intercom button and immediately his loyal assistant came on the line, "Yes, sir?"

"Mary, please contact the White House and tell them I need five minutes with the President."

"Yes, sir."

He grabbed his coat and called down for a car. He was on his way to see POTUS, the President of The United States, Cerab Hussein.

Chapter Three

Clarisse Dubois stepped out of the taxi, her short cocktail dress riding high up her thigh, and paid the leering driver. She liked to walk the last couple of blocks towards her apartment in the Montparnasse section of Paris, especially now, this early May morning, when the air was filled with the scent of jasmines and roses. Her apartment was on a one way side street and it added Euros to the taxi fare to go around the block to drop her directly in front of her building.

It was brisk when the sun went down but she loved this time of year. She was happy that at four a.m. her day was finally over. The previous night was like many that had come before. It was spent in the company of dull, boring rich men. She was used to them standing taller and leering down her dress, trying to catch a glimpse of her cleavage and well shaped young breasts.

But Clarisse was not familiar with the Arab custom of constantly talking business in Egyptian, Sudanese, Farsi language or whatever else they were speaking. Continuing to smile, she waited for them to finish so she could leave and go home. But she had been paid well for the night.

Not too bad, she thought, reviewing the evening in her mind, *at least they had great food.* The evening had been worth it, for she had made some good money, just smiling and laughing with these old men— and not on her back, which was fine with her.

So distracted in thought, she did not notice the man who had followed her from the corner where the taxi dropped her.

She missed her Hakim and was excited to talk with him earlier in the week after he arrived back in Washington, DC on his way home to Baltimore. She had to only wait another three weeks before he would return to Paris. Perhaps they could then picnic again in the park by the Seine. She so enjoyed a picnic by the slow river that ran through Paris. They would lie in each other's arms underneath the tall dragging branches of the willow trees on the isle in the middle of the scenic river.

A shuffling noise sounded behind her, interrupting her thoughts of an idyllic picnic by the river. She walked a little faster, shot a glance over her shoulder, checking, while she fumbled for the tear gas spray-gun in her purse. A man in a dark business suit, tall and slight, with hair the color of night and carrying a briefcase, walked rather intently but he did not seem to be paying much attention to her.

He crossed to the other side of the street and she made her way inside her iron gate, running up the steps of her apartment building. The outside of her building was full of deep shadows. The streetlight was flickering off and on in front of her building and she made a mental note to call the building manager the next day to have it fixed.

She pulled the house keys from the outside pocket of her purse and was soon safe inside. Once there, Clarisse breathed a sigh of relief for she had remembered that some of the other girls had encountered many over eager "clients." They would follow them home to offer them more money for massages or extended pleasures.

Clarisse was tired and only wanted to soak in the tub. It had been a very long day. She sat at her desk and pulled out the business cards she'd accumulated over the last two days and decided to file them tomorrow. *Never know when you may need a contact or two.*

She checked for messages. No message from Hakim on either her machine or her cell phone, but then she remembered the time zone difference. He was probably still in bed, hopefully alone, she chuckled to herself. She unbuttoned her sheer silk blouse in the hallway, while making her way towards the kitchen refrigerator to pour some wine before running her bath water and relaxing. Tomorrow she would sleep in. What a relief.

She did not bother turning on other lights, for she knew the layout of the apartment by heart. The light from the moon and the flickering streetlight shone its whitish yellow light through her front windows, allowing her to navigate her way.

Her apartment was large and rather lavish by Parisian standards, with four tall front windows, one large bedroom with ornate wall panels lining the hallway to the bedroom. Hakim fell in love with it the first day he saw it and signed the papers for her on the spot. It had become his home away from home when not in the States or traveling in the Mideast. She missed him more than she cared to admit.

The young, part-time model perused the contents of the fridge and was pleased to see that she still had some red wine left over from her visitor evenings before. She poured a large glass and re-corked the vintage wine bottle, shoving it into the rear of the fridge, then grabbed the last orange off the shelf.

She did not see or hear him until she closed the refrigerator door. It was the man who followed her to her building. She gasped and dropped her wine and orange at the sight of him, both crashing to the floor. Before she could scream, the knife was quickly at her throat and his hand gripped the hair at the back of her head.

"My money is in my purse, there on the chair in the foyer. Take it all! Just leave me alone, please." She wanted to cry but she was afraid that was just what he wanted. She held her tears and her fear in check. He raised the knife, glistening from the soft light of the moon outside coming through the side window and pointed it at her, motioning her toward the bedroom.

She did not recognize him from tonight's affair or any other for that matter. She thought hard, trying to remember if she had seen him somewhere, but no luck. Her pace quickened as she looked for a place to run and hide. The bathroom, but it was at the other end of the hall, behind her.

His silence was unusual for they all seemed to want to talk. He was different. Her fears grew as they walked quietly through her apartment. She could yell but that might only enrage him.

Clarisse led the way into the bedroom and felt this was the one place she was in control, even though he had the knife, and still held her by her hair. He watched her every move. She recognized the long knife as one from her kitchen.

When they reached the bed she turned to face him, her blouse totally unbuttoned and her breasts swaying in the soft light of the room. It did not seem to catch his attention. At age twenty-nine, sexy, pretty and well built, she was in the flower of her youth. She had men pretty well figured out—they were all the same. She knew what he wanted.

He pointed toward the bed, now dangling four yellow silk ropes from the serrated knife blade. He motioned her to lie down. Now she knew exactly what he wanted, he wanted control. She knew his type. Most times they would tie you up, sit in a chair and be pleasured by the mere fact of having a woman lying helpless before him. She caressed the bright cutting edge with her finger as she pulled the yellow silk ties from his weapon. She knew the drill.

She tied both of her ankles to the posts at the foot of the bed, and then she tied one of her wrists to the headboard. The other wrist she left untied waiting for him to complete his fantasy. She faked a moan, trying to get this over with as quickly as possible, so he would leave and she could finish her warm bath and pour another glass of wine. He tied the last rope then put duct tape over her mouth. It was only then she noticed he wore light green surgical gloves.

He came close and sat next to her on the bed, stroking her hair, parting her blouse with the knife tip, admiring her well endowed female anatomy. A red crescent star tattoo graced his right wrist at the base. She had seen many of those tattoos this evening on the bodyguards of the guests tonight, but she dare not ask its meaning.

She searched his eyes and was terrified to see staring back at her, eyes containing no emotion or passion. His eyes were black, like a shark's before an attack. Fear rose in her throat again as she approached unknown territory. He was not like the others.

His hand slid down her stomach and parted her legs, slowly cutting off her lace panties before he laid the knife on the bedside table. She tensed her body and he moved closer to her, reached under her head as if to kiss her. She lay there beneath him, helpless, but acting like she wanted him when in reality what she wanted was for it all to be over. She had difficulty breathing only through her nose. Her breaths were coming to her quicker, shallower.

He was still fully dressed when he removed a pillow from beneath her head, he leaned closer, so close he could smell the Chanel perfume she'd dabbed between her breasts. She raised her hips slightly from the bed, waiting, resigned to her fate. Smiling, totally in control, he took the pillow from beneath her head and suddenly pressed it over her face, pushing down hard. She shook her body to the left then to the right, trying to get free. She tried to scream but her voice was muffled. She tried to call out for help but the screams were trapped from release by the heavy tape. She tried to get free. She needed air, fresh air, heavenly air.

Her body twisted while she squirmed fiercely to be rid of the pillow that was drawing the life from her. She couldn't breathe. His strong arms held the pillow firmly in place. Her nose and mouth were covered, she'd lost all control and panicked as she realized what was happening. She was bound tight with the silk strands by her own hand. How stupid she was!

She was gasping for air but found none. She tried to take a breath through her nose but no matter how she tried she could not get away from the smothering pillow. She was too young to die! Her last thoughts were of Hakim and how she missed him. Then, spent, her body went limp.

Jasara left the pillow on her lifeless body. His pulse rate never raised, he was calm as if he were sitting reading. He surveyed the room, seeking any telltale signs of his presence or clues that he'd ever been there. When he found none, he walked towards the front door of the apartment, peeling the abandoned orange, no longer needed by its former owner. When police found the body they would think the obvious, a sex play gone wrong and not an execution or as his employer liked to call it, an inoculation.

He strolled past the just opening crepe restaurants, raising their shutters releasing the sweet smell of crepes lofting just so in the air. The street cleaners hummed in their relentless task of keeping the streets of Paris clean. The tall thin man hailed a taxi at Rue de Rennes and headed for the airport, just as a light rain began to sprinkle the early morning streets of Paris.

He headed to the airport. He'd been busy the last couple of days, flying in from Istanbul the day before, Cairo the day before that and Indonesia before that, where it all started. He was on his way to Washington, DC and the next name on his list. He knew that time was money as he hurried to his next rendezvous. He unfolded the heavy blue paper containing his list while the taxi made quick headway to Charles de Gaulle Airport in the early morning traffic. The next name on the list was a familiar one. He smiled, with this one he would need to be very delicate. He was running out of time.

Chapter Four

Eduarte Manizales was glad the rain finally stopped and the sun was shining again in his adopted home city of Buenos Aires. He could now close his guitar shop for his traditional lunch and wander over to the Plaza Dorrego for the next two hours. He liked it here, except for the rainy season. It was a very low key city with good restaurants, lots of music, dancing and plenty of pretty women. His kind of place.

Manizales was a big man, topping the scale at well over three-hundred pounds and he loved to eat. The short walk from the shop to the square had him drenched with sweat even though the temperature was in the seventies, unusually warm for May in Argentina. After the rain stopped the steam returned but it was worth it. He loved the sights and sounds of this southern city and the relaxed atmosphere that came with it. The scent of afternoon meals filled the air and made his stomach growl. Most locals had their main meal later at night but he liked a big lunch, and a big dinner.

He made his way through the now bustling square, past the silver stalls and all the young boys hawking subscriptions to magazines. "No, *gracias*," was his usual response. He soon found himself at his local favorite, *Tango Puerto*, The Door to Tango.

Manizales had tried to learn Spanish upon his arrival in Buenos Aires years ago but had little luck, so he just gave up. He let his wallet speak for him instead.

"*Buenos dias, Senor Manizales.* We have missed you the last couple of days. We hope all is well with you."

"*Si, Raphael.* All is well. I have been traveling and with this weather its been hard to get out. Terrible rain."

"*Si Senor*, but we missed you nonetheless. Let me prepare your favorite meal, *Puchero*, our specialty."

"Wonderful," replied the big man. "In the meantime Raphael, *vino, rouge, por favor*."

Puchero. It was just a meat and vegetable stew, but they gave him very large portions with lots of homemade fresh bread, so he was happy. He could sit and watch the young ones Tango directly in front of him. The women all dressed in black and the men with slicked back hair. They would dance for hours and he never seemed to tire of watching the Latin dance and the women in tight tops, skirts hiked high on their legs.

He eased his heavy weight into a nearby chair that if it could talk would ask him to go elsewhere. The chair squeaked loudly under his considerable heft, but he soon made himself comfortable under the white umbrella which blocked the noon day sun.

Ah, its been a hot Argentine summer and I'm ready for Autumn. He opened the newspaper on the checkerboard table cloth, then glanced around to see if his wine was coming soon.

"*Raphael, vino!*" he called as a reminder.

"*Si Senor Manziales*, coming right up," replied the old shop keeper, while his son hustled through the café to bring the wine.

Reading through the paper Eduarte thought back to his rather strange conversation with his old friend Hakim. *Why would Hakim want to know all of that information?* It'd been years since he had left the TMSFS (Tehran Medical School of Further Studies), their subterfuge for the Iranian biological weapons program.

Hakim was his confidant and co-worker for so many years and then to hear from him suddenly out of the blue, was unsettling. If he could be found by Hakim, then anyone could find him. Maybe he needed to take a vacation far, far away. Hakim was the best researcher, nobody did it better. He was a strange one though. You never knew whose side he was on, but everybody came to him seeking help and advice.

The big man folded the newspaper in half and read the sports scores. The dancers were starting their Tango. This was what he enjoyed about Buenos Aires the most. Dancers set up their music and temporary dance floors and would dance an impromptu Tango on a street corner, along with the ever present hat to accept donations.

Off to Eduarte's left and three tables behind, a quiet man nonchalantly read the same newspaper as Manizales. The man had his target in his sights and it was only a matter of time before he would pull the noose tighter. He'd finished his lunch earlier and was waiting, just waiting, drinking mango flavored water, the way the locals drank it. His name was Carlos Scarlatti, a former hit man and mob enforcer from New Jersey.

Carlos was tall and rather handsome, with neatly groomed short curly black hair, and sharp facial features which he got from his mother. His mother was of royal Ethiopian descent and his father was from Uruguay, where Carlos grew up after his mother died in childbirth. His chin always appeared to have a grubby stubble shading of hair which was impossible to remove due to his dark complexion.

Sitting in the restaurant one would notice his suit was slightly snug on his biceps, a dead giveaway he was a committed body builder. But he blended in with his stylish haircut and European cut clothes and his dark, dashing appearance in this cosmopolitan South American city of Buenos Aires. Handsome, he could have easily found work as a model, but life had dealt him different cards.

Scarlatti's father arranged for illegal immigrants to be transported to the United States. Carlos had been sent to New York City by his father to collect a debt from a man and his family who were sent to America, but failed to pay the rest of the money to his father. He had dispatched his large son to find them and make an example of them. It was bad for business if illegal immigrants did not pay their bills.

Carlos caught up with them in New Jersey but got caught by the police burying their bodies in a field behind their house. He was arrested and sent to jail until one of the New Jersey mob bosses Marti

Romano heard about it. Marti got him released on a technicality after paying some large bribes to his friends in high places.

He worked for Romano as an enforcer for three years, gaining a reputation as an efficient killer who worked cool under pressure, until he got caught in the back of an RV in bed with Romano's wife and was forced to take flight. He was still looking over his shoulders every time he was in an airport—the easiest place to be detected for someone in his business. Now he worked as an international freelance hit man to the highest bidder and the pay was very, very good. Fifty thousand a hit allowed him to live a life of luxury on the Caribbean island of Saint Thomas.

Carlos' white linen suit coolly comforted him in the noon day Buenos Aires sun while he shooed away the ever present hawkers who were selling everything from candy, lottery tickets, fruit to silver buckles. The young kids had been without sales for nearly four days due to rain chasing off their customers and now they swarmed like mosquitoes especially around anyone sitting still.

He rubbed his aching eyes, now pounding with an image and he saw an all too familiar vision. He saw himself walking down a long corridor and a big man in tan suit leaning on a wall in a bathroom with black and white tile. He next saw the man lying on the floor, his dead stare penetrating his soul, the life leaving him as blood oozed from his head, his heart beating towards its final pump.

Carlos Scarlatti rubbed his eyes harder to make the vision and headache go away. He had visions of the future. When he first told people of his hidden talent they all laughed so he remained silent from then on, but the visions of his future hits came back all the same.

The server brought a fresh garden salad with tangerines and avocados to Manizales' table, "*Bueno?*" asked the elder proprietor.

"*Si*, everything you do is always good."

"*Caballeros, por favor?*" Carlos asked, walking towards the old restaurant owner, seeking directions to the men's restroom. On his return he saw a double portion of *Puchero*, on the counter waiting to be served to the large man outside. He removed his hat and fanned his face with the wide brim, obscuring the view of the *Puchero* from everyone in the restaurant before returning to his seat outside. He knew it was only a matter of time before the big man would get up to relieve himself. Now Carlos would wait, one thing he had learned was that to be a successful assassin one must have patience.

He did not like making his hits in daylight and around so many people, but his clients had insisted that the hits on the list be accomplished as quickly as possible and they had given him a bonus to do so, doubling his usual fee. He did not have the luxury of time to study the comings and goings of his target like he usually preferred and then be able to meticulously plan the hit, because time was of the essence. In his mind the client was always right, at least this client was but he still did not like it.

Carlos returned to his seat and watched the Tango activity in the Plaza. This was his kind of city. *Maybe I should move here and retire. With this contract I would have all of the money I need. Not a bad idea.* He could bring his boat here and disappear.

Scarlatti watched the waiter serve the big man his meal and waited for the man to consume large quantities of wine to wash it down.

"Ah, there it is, my *Puchero*," said his favorite patron, now famished at not having eaten in over three hours. He gulped it down as fast as he could, without reason, hardly even taking a breath.

"Oh, so good. You have outdone yourself," he said to the owner before delving back into his delectable meal. He drank and drank the unending supply of wine and soon he stood up and staggered towards the restroom at the rear of the restaurant.

Boy I don't know what happened to me, Eduarte thought, leaning against the bathroom wall as the door opened behind him. "*Occupiedo,*" he uttered loudly to the intruder, as he relieved himself. He did not hear the door close. "*Occupiedo,*" he repeated again, perturbed that someone would stay in the room when being told it was occupied. Then, he felt the cold steel of a Berretta revolver positioned at the base of his neck.

Manziales heard one pop but was dead by the time the second one was quietly discharged into his collapsed body on the black and white tile bathroom floor. .

Dead on the floor. Carlos' trademark, two slugs to the head, one for good measure.

Carlos fixed his tie and his hat in the mirror before leaving through the rear entrance of the cafe, past the disabled security camera and down the long narrow alleyway that populated downtown Buenos Aires. He hailed a taxi at the other end of the Dorrego Plaza past Bolivar Boulevard. "The Ezeiza International Airport please," he said to the young driver.

"American? I have a cousin in Chicago," the cab driver stated rather than asked. They all had cousins in Chicago, thought Carlos.

"You know Chicago? Maybe you know my cousin, Simon Ceasoral, he is an electrician."

"I'm Canadian, from Montreal," he replied coolly and opened his newspaper as he settled in for the short ride to the airport. In the rear seat of the cab he leaned back waiting for the air conditioning to finally cool the back of the taxi. He set the newspaper aside and unfolded the heavy blue bonded paper to review the names on his list, even though he had looked at his list a dozen times before.

Carlos had only two more hits, with his next stop being in Baltimore and then on to Washington, DC. *At least it wasn't New Jersey*, he said smugly to himself but it still made him nervous being back in Baltimore. It was too close to New Jersey and Romano's reach for his comfort. He would get in, get out and then head back to Saint Thomas and retire for good.

It had been a hectic last couple of days but he'd been paid well, very well. He took a flight to Mexico City and booked a tourist shopping bus from Juarez to Las Cruces, New Mexico, to avoid detection. When they stopped in New Mexico, he broke away from the group and headed for the airport and a flight to Houston before he boarded an American Airlines flight to Baltimore. They probably would not still be searching for him but he felt he was better off safe than sorry. He wished his assignments were over but he still had work to do. He looked at his list. The next name on the list was Palmer, Richard Palmer in Baltimore. He was next on the list to die.

Chapter Five

The Season, as the locals called it, was over in Palm Beach County and all the wealthy snowbirds and socialites had flown on to their next nesting destination up North and out West. You could now get a parking spot anywhere you chose, have dinner without making a reservation and encounter no lines at the supermarket. The weather in early May was faultless, warm, and sunny and every day was a Chamber of Commerce perfect kind of day in paradise.

Nick Ryan stirred from his bed hearing the coffee maker go off in the kitchen, making its final gasping, wheezing noise as it squeezed the last drop of moisture from the reservoir. Steam and the strong smell of Brazilian hardwood coffee wandered through his oceanfront apartment.

The breeze coming off the ocean and the scent of salt air stirred through the open crack in the sliding glass doors in his apartment above Caffé Luna Rosa. The slight breeze caused the sheer curtains to part which covered the wide glass doors.

His apartment was on the top floor over the restaurant and if you didn't mind the sound of people talking and laughing at ten thirty at night, it was the ideal penthouse apartment. It was right across the street from the beach at the end of bustling Atlantic Avenue right on Beach Route A1A, in the quaint little town of Delray Beach. The apartment next to his was occupied but he had not met the other tenant, even though Nick had been there for over a month.

Caffe Luna Rosa was one of many busy and hip restaurants on A1A facing the beach, but it was the only one which had rental apartments above them. His father was the one who remembered seeing the rental sign during dinner one evening. Nick had been forced to vacate his father's beach bungalow where he was visiting after a rogue wave flooded out their fifty-year old surfside cottage. The contractors seemed to take forever to finish the reconstruction job, aided in part by the Palm Beach County building inspectors. They were not crazy about a house built that close to the ocean and while they could not deny a permit, they did everything in their power to slow down the process.

For over a month Nick's father had been recuperating from surgery on his back to remove a long time bullet fragment which had moved dangerously close to his spine. Now he was in a special rehab facility in Boynton Beach, fifteen minutes away.

Nick rolled over in bed and was greeted by the smiling picture of Katie, his wonderful, but now deceased, wife. He looked at the photo longingly and said good morning. She did not return the hello. God, did he still love her and oh how much he missed her. He could hear her calling him to join her. Whoever said that grief got easier with time was wrong, dead wrong.

Katie's picture was placed strategically on the side table at his bedside, next to a scrap of paper containing the only haunting clue to her brutal murder. It was a yellow handwritten sheet of paper with the names Jessie and Linda with a series of numbers starting with 561, the area code for South Florida. The phone number belonged to no one. The other numbers were a mystery too. Jessie and Linda were ghosts, nowhere to be found.

Other numbers were scattered on the small scrap of yellow paper. He could not find their names in Katie's cell phone, home phone, office, rolodex, computer, Blackberry, nothing. He had even searched through her desk at her office in Baltimore at the Theoretical Applied Physics Lab (TAPL). No luck. Nick continued to search for other clues for over a year. He was at a dead end, finished. Nothing.

He opened the drawer to the bedside table to begin his daily ritual. Nick reached inside and pulled out the black and silver police special. He wrapped his fingers around the cool indifferent pistol, a Smith and Wesson .45 caliber, with only one bullet loaded in the chamber. He spun the cylinder around like a wheel of fortune and after kissing the picture of his beloved Katie, he placed the revolver to his forehead and pulled the trigger. A loud click echoed throughout the apartment. He was spared to live another day. *Maybe he should spin again or add another bullet.*

His thinking was distracted by the sound of a female voice just outside his apartment, through his sliding patio door, speaking what sounded like fluent Italian. He threw on an old pair of lifeguard beach trunks over his boxers, slid on a t-shirt and grabbed his coffee. The traffic noise was picking up outside and he checked the time on his alarm clock, with the cracked glass front panel, it was eight-fifteen a.m.

Nick pushed aside the sheer drape that sailed in the breeze and stepped outside to the cool morning Florida sunshine, just another glorious day in paradise. The sound of the voice grew louder as he approached the end of the balcony. On the porch next door sitting in a chair was a woman with a pair of gorgeous, athletic legs. She wore a tight fitting expensive silk jacket like Katie used to favor. Long shoulder length auburn hair, with huge gorgeous curls caressed her neck but her back was to him and he could not make out her face. *Lord, let her face match the rest of the package,* he said to himself, as he leaned on the railing overlooking the street below, cradling his old FBI coffee mug between his hands.

She was still talking on the phone when she stood up and turned around, gesticulating with her hands. Yeah, she had to be Italian. It was then that she finally noticed him. Slightly startled at first but then, looking directly at Nick, she smiled. She finally blew a kiss into the phone and said, "*Nonna addio*, bye Grandma," before turning her attention to Nick.

"Good Morning, neighbor." She grinned and held up her phone. "My grandmother is from the old country and doesn't speak English too well. I try to help but what can you do?"

Nick grinned in response.

She picked up her coffee mug and walked towards him and along the divider that separated the two balconies. "I'm Rose, Rose Scalese but everyone calls me Rosa." She smiled, while cautiously surveying him up and down. She liked what she saw.

"Nick, Nick Ryan," he replied. The cars below them had stopped, blasting their horns probably waiting to stake their claim for a prized beach parking spot.

"I haven't seen you before this," she said. She was tall and her high heels made her appear that much taller. She must have been a model at some point for her facial features were soft as if you could touch them with your eyes and her clothes were ideally tailored and color coordinated. Her figure matched her attire perfectly from everything he could see.

"I've been doing some traveling, up and down the East Coast," he stammered as she unbuttoned her fitted jacket revealing both a Glock pistol on her hip along with her police ID dangling from her neck, hidden before by her jacket. But his attention was soon diverted elsewhere. He was right; she was well built, very well built.

"Let me officially welcome you to the neighborhood," she said, as she saw him eyeing her badge and weapon. "I'm with the DEA, Southern District. I hear you work at the Bureau."

Nick did not immediately respond. He did not like to talk about his work at the FBI. He'd worked there over five years before taking a leave of absence last year after his beloved Katie was murdered.

"I was, but I am officially on a temporary leave of absence now."

Since he joined the FBI, he had lost his mother, his older brother, his wife and now he looked after his father recovering from a bullet lodged close to his spine. He did not blame the Bureau for his troubles but he also did not believe in coincidences.

"Join me for dinner tonight? My treat?" Rosa asked, changing the subject.

"Sure. Where and when?"

"How about meeting at City Oyster Restaurant on Atlantic Avenue, down on restaurant row? Say seven?"

"Sounds great," he told her. "You don't want to do the cafe downstairs?"

"No. Not tonight. I would love some fresh fish."

"Okay. City Oyster it is then."

She turned to leave but thinking better of it stopped and faced Nick. "Oh Nick, no offense, it's not a fancy place but you will have to shower and shave. Some fresh clothes without coffee stains would also go a long way for us getting a decent table." She smiled, her eyes twinkling with humor. "By the way, I'm named after the Rosa in Caffe Luna Rosa. My parents were good friends with the owners. See ya tonight, Nick."

"Rosa, don't worry. They tell me I clean up pretty good. See you tonight," he said with a chuckle.

She walked away but turned halfway around to get another look at him. She waved before disappearing out of sight.

Nick hummed the haunting melody, "*The Hills of Yesterday*," the theme to the movie *The Molly Maguire's* which he'd watched the night before, while he headed down the back stairs, across the street and out onto the beach for his morning jog. It was time to check on how the reconstruction was going with his father's beach bungalow. He was looking forward to it being finished and moving back in with his Dad. It was the closest thing to feeling like home. Technically, home was Baltimore, but that was a long way from here both geographically and emotionally. He closed up their house in Baltimore after Katie died and then left for Florida. He had not been back since.

His usual jog down the beach made for a good run. It usually felt good to run on the beach, to hear the surf pounding on the shore and feel the splash of salt spray in his face. Jogging down the beach, he was usually joined by other early morning joggers. But today there was no one, and his thoughts wondered. Maybe his life could change. Maybe it wasn't too late. He missed his Katie. God did he miss her.

He finished his jog. Time to shower. He stripped off his clothes, but once again his thoughts were hijacked by the names of Jessie and Linda. Who the hell were they? And what did they have to do with Katie's death? He would find out, regardless of how long it took him. The Smith and Wesson .45 lured him to the side table, with its cold, come-hither smile. The cold steel weapon felt warm in his hand. He felt lucky today…

Chapter Six

The city of Delray Beach for years had been just like all of the other quaint beachside towns up and down the Atlantic Coast, with beautiful beaches, hotels, tourists and snowbirds. Things changed years back when restaurant owner, John Great bought large sections of rundown properties on the main street in town, Atlantic Avenue. They were located far from the beach and he started renovating them two and three buildings at a time.

Great created a holding company, modestly called, Great Time Restaurant Group. He opened his first restaurant in Delray, City Oyster which featured a great menu, outdoor dining, and wonderfully fresh seafood. It attracted nationwide attention after a *USA Today* article appeared in the paper touting the renaissance he created. The gold rush was on and soon Atlantic Avenue sprouted up new restaurants, shops, boutiques and art galleries on every corner becoming a mecca for foodies and snowbirds.

New condo buildings soon followed, built by the dozen and then the banks, hotels and other retail shops soon followed. The stretch of land further East on Atlantic retained its old world charm but soon it sprouted a colossal JW Beachfront Hotel and four or five restaurants opened facing the beach right on the beach road. Caffe Luna Rosa was one of those. It was a sea of calm near the beach but not far from the maddening crowds of downtown Delray.

On most nights the streets were crowded with people strolling under the South Florida stars, enjoying the benefits of the beautiful warm spring nights before the rainy season began. It truly was a paradise.

Nick Ryan jumped into his jeep and drove down Atlantic Avenue cruising the quiet section of Delray over the inter-coastal waterway past restaurant row that lined the busy section of the street. He took the Interstate-95 North exit and headed towards Boynton Beach, where his father was convalescing. The wind felt good in his hair as he raced up the highway.

As a family growing up they moved around quite a bit because of his father's work with the Bureau. They were always relocating from one city to another but his father's overseas assignments were the toughest for Nick. They could not always go with his father due to the risks involved.

Nick followed the family tradition, like his older brother Chad and his father, attending Penn State, playing football, enlisting in the Marine Corp the day after graduation. He spent four years in the Marine Expeditionary Force before being discharged. He went to work for The FBI after taking six months off and traveling to see the country.

"I have seen the world but I have not seen America," he fondly remembered saying to his father. Joining the Bureau was the proudest day of his life, only surpassed by the day of his wedding to Katie. He worked undercover with the Fraud Unit and then he volunteered for the Anti-Terrorist Investigation Team (AIT) and knew then he had found a home.

Nick pulled off I-95 at the Boynton Beach exit, and headed towards the private facility off of Jog Road called Stevens Resident Rehab, where his dad was staying during his recovery.

Surgery on Nick's father's back had always been ruled out as being too risky but the bullet had shifted and put pressure on a nerve causing him to lose all control of his legs. The decision was made and finally the surgery was performed two weeks earlier but he was still confined to a wheelchair until given the final clearance from the doctors. That was the one difference between him and his father, his father had no patience.

"Hey Pop, how the hell are you?" Nick proclaimed after seeing his father sitting by the window glancing at his watch in his private room. The facility was partially funded by the Bureau as a "safe" facility for rehabbing key employees away from public and prying eyes. It had all the outward appearances of a senior center except for the dark suited, gun toting guards inside the front and rear entrance and the state of the art surveillance system.

"You're late."

"Hey, I'm right on time," said Nick, glancing at his watch, showing the time to his father.

"If you are not ten minutes early you are late, remember?"

If Nick didn't know he was in a medical facility he wouldn't have known it from the room. Wood paneled, a small cluttered desk in the corner, plush green carpeting and three sets of drapes covering the bulletproof glass windows.

Frank Ryan shoved the chess board towards his son and put two tumbler glasses with ice on the small table between them. His son closed the door and pulled the bottle of Jack Daniels from the brown paper bag pouring generously, leaving room for a splash of ginger ale.

"What do you want to play, white or black?" his father asked him, taking a tall swig of the Kentucky sipping whiskey, making a frown at his son's habit of diluting the drink with ginger ale.

"I'll take white." He usually liked playing the black chess pieces, starting second but today he felt lucky.

"You feel lucky today, huh?"

"Yeah, I do."

His father looked tired. Nick made a mental note to see the doctors and talk about getting him out of there, if only for a day.

"I went by the cottage today and it is moving along pretty good."

His father perked up, as Nick knew he would. "Yeah? When is it going to be finished? You get to live right at the beach above Luna Rosa and I get stuck here. I have seniority, I should have gotten the beach pad."

"You are the one who needed surgery remember? And besides I am better lookin' then you and I won the coin toss." His father started laughing so hard he began to cough. Nick did not always know which buttons to press for his Dad but today he'd hit the exact one to keep his spirits up.

They played three games, his father winning them all before he pushed away from the table and leaned back to look at his son who boxed up the chess set and put it in the closet.

Frank Ryan keenly watched his son. Nick Ryan had his mother's blue grey eyes, curly blond hair, gentle but strong temperament but the Robert Redford good looks and muscular physique obviously came from his father. Katie used to say that Nick could walk through a restaurant and all the women would be looking at him, undressing him with their eyes but he was oblivious to it all. He was a good husband and a good son, he could be counted on.

Father and son sat back easy in their chairs, looking at the Florida sun making another gorgeous day of it. Sometimes they sat for hours, doing nothing, just enjoying each other's company which was originally tough for Nick's impatient father, but now he looked forward to these quiet times. Must be getting older, Nick thought.

"So how are you doing?" his father asked, breaking the silence.

"I'm good. The Bureau still sends me email updates on things and even though I am on leave I still feel involved."

"That's not what I meant."

"I know dad. They say its gets easier with time but I don't know if that's true."

"You have to get on with your life. Put it behind you. I did."

Nick's mother had been shot execution style while Nick and Frank were on an overseas duty assignment in Indonesia. She was found naked, with her hands and ankles bound together behind her back, a single bullet lodged in her brain. Frank kept the bullet hanging around his neck as a constant reminder.

There had been one clue to the murder. Frank and Nick pursued the lead together unofficially for nearly a year, before finally giving up. Years later Nick had to deal with the murder of his darling Katie and was not able to find her killer either. He was still haunted by both deaths.

"I will the day you throw the bullet away. I miss Katie terribly."

"I know you do. But you have to get on with your life. That's what Katie would have wanted. Have you gotten laid or at least dated since Katie's death?"

"Pop!"

"Well, have you?"

"As a matter of fact I have a date tonight with a beautiful woman, and she's a cop."

"Bullshit. What happened, you get pulled over at a traffic stop and you pleaded your way out for a dinner?"

"No, she's DEA. I just met her and as a matter of fact I have to head out and get some new clothes and rush to get home to shower, shave and change."

"What's her name?" asked his father, still not sure if his son was telling him the truth.

"Rosa Scalese, if it's any of your business."

"Sounds mob connected. You say she's a cop?"

"Yeah, DEA. Gotta go, Pop. I'll see you in few days." He kissed his father on the forehead, and headed towards the door.

"Ask her if she has any friends that might be interested in an old cop."

Nick waved his hand over his shoulder, heading for his rendezvous. The fact that the two best investigators for the FBI both had their most precious loved ones taken away from them was unspoken, but always on their mind.

Nick got to City Oyster Restaurant early and nabbed a prime outdoor table on the corner by the sidewalk. He had just put the menus and wine list down on the table when he saw Rosa walking down the street, looking gorgeous. She walked the calm easy walk of someone who was not in a hurry and knew exactly where they were headed. She was dressed for the sometimes cool nights of South Florida with a beige sweater over her shoulders, tied in front, the French way.

"I grabbed a table outside, I hope you don't mind?" He stood up to greet her.

"Fine," she replied warmly, with an electric smile and leaned forward to give him a hello kiss on his cheek. She smelled of Chanel and her silk blouse was slightly opaque, for Nick could see the subtle lace pattern of her bra through it. Unbuttoned from the top, just the right amount of buttons…three.

Nick had a theory about women and blouse buttons. If they were totally buttoned they were just like their buttons, uptight and buttoned up. If they had one button unbuttoned, they were your normal everyday gal. Two buttons meant a run of the mill adventurer. Three buttons meant sexy, very adventuresome and someone who could handle most things. More than three buttons, was too many, and meant a stripper or someone desperate for attention.

After they ordered and the drinks arrived, Rosa toasted, "Welcome to the neighborhood." She gave him a huge comfortable smile and her eyes twinkled. Rosa reminded him of Katie, with her gracious ways, easy smile and relaxed demeanor.

"Thanks," he responded with cheer. He was torn. She was the first woman he'd spent time with since Katie died and a shiver of unfaithful guilt crept into his inner thoughts. He tried to dismiss them, to banish them to the dark recesses of his mind, but they continued to return to haunt him.

"You were right. You clean up real good," she said admiringly. "So, what do you do to keep yourself busy, Nick?"

"I'd been staying with my Dad at his beach house after he needed surgery. I've been taking care of him for the last couple of months. We got flooded out of our beach house, so I rented the place at Luna Rosa's while they fix it. I also do some freelance investigating for some insurance company friends of mine, just to keep busy."

"Is your Dad at Stevens, in Boynton Beach?"

"Yeah, not a very well kept Bureau secret I guess."

"No." She smiled. He knew what she wanted to ask him but was searching for an opening in which to insert her question. They talked a while, sipping on their wine and watching the city start to come alive.

She finally asked, "How long since you have been away from the Bureau, Nick?"

"I took a leave a little over a year ago, right after my wife died."

"It's been tough I guess."

"Yeah."

"You still miss her a lot, huh?"

"Yeah," he said starting to retreat inside himself.

"What do you think about?"

His eyes narrowed as he looked up from his meal and laid down his fork, avoiding her question. "What exactly do you do with the DEA?"

Her eyes registered disappointment. "I only thought it would help to talk to someone, Nick. Please don't be angry with me."

"You're a shrink aren't you?"

"Nick, I only…"

"Why didn't you just tell me you needed a clinical guinea pig? I would have made it a lot easier on both of us. I am fine and I certainly don't need to talk to someone like you." He got up, tossed down a few twenties and then walked away from the table. She caught up with him just as he reached his car at the now deserted parking lot on Second Avenue.

"Nick, I'm sorry. I should have been more up front with you. My father told me a little of what he knew and he was concerned that you may harm yourself and asked me to talk to you. That's all, really." She touched his shoulder. "She must have been something else to have this impact on you."

"My life is in the crapper because some creep murdered my wife and me, the big hot shot FBI investigator can't find him."

"Nick you will feel better, I promise you."

He turned his full fury on her as he spun around, throwing her hard against the car door, pinning her to the car with his forearm underneath her neck with his other hand holding her arms behind her back.

"It won't get better. It hasn't gotten better, believe me. There is not a day that goes by that I don't remember what happened. Not only did they strip her of all of her clothes, rape her—my wife, the most beautiful woman in my world—they then put two slugs in her head, cut off her hands then they left me a cryptic message which keeps me up every night trying to solve its crazy meaning."

His lips trembled, holding back tears. "I could not even have the closure of an open casket at her funeral. Will I get over it, yeah someday, but I don't need you sticking your shrink nose into my personal affairs. Leave me alone." He let her loose, leaving her gasping for air. He started his car and was gone.

Rosa stood watching his car drive away, even more concerned.

Nick stopped at the bar, Boston's On the Beach next to Luna Rosa and began to drink himself into oblivion. He stumbled up his back steps and made his way to his apartment. Sitting on the bed he looked at the picture of him holding Katie, his arms wrapped around her, protecting her. *Some protector I turned out to be. What good am I? He never realized how tiny she was compared to him, as he held her in his arms.*

He saw the names, Jessie and Linda and numbers on the yellow sheet of paper, mocking him, as if to say, *catch me if you can.*

He opened the drawer and retrieved his old friend, howling silently for him, his Smith and Wesson service revolver. Spinning the cylinder, he placed the barrel to his forehead, just where Katie's bullet hole had been. He pulled the trigger once. *Click.* He pulled the trigger again.

Chapter Seven

"POTUS is on the move," said Agent Miller speaking into a microphone in his sleeve from inside the conference room and within moments the doors swung open wide. The first to appear was Phil Muth, a senior OPP Secret Service agent, all dressed in black with a heavily starched white shirt and a narrow black tie and the ever-present sunglasses. Everyone outside of the unit joked that OPP looked like the characters from the movie, *Men in Black*.

The agents belonged to the Office of Presidential Protection (OPP), a specialty unit within the Secret Service itself. The President moved smoothly in the safety of the White House corridors shadowed by members of the Secret Service and the OPP. After the assassination attempt by John Hinckley on the life of President Ronald Reagan, the Secret Service formed a specialized protective unit whose main job was to encircle the president and ensure his personal safety.

The OPP was staffed by the most loyal and rabidly dedicated members of the Secret Service. While the Secret Service was responsible for coordinating Presidential travel, logistics and safety it was the OPP who was the top dog when it came to protecting the President.

This small elite unit had personal responsibility for the protection of the President and his family. They worked outside of the Secret Service organization, having their own communications, budget and staffing parameters. They also were the unit that handled the secret Presidential Target List, which were individuals targeted worldwide for elimination or assassination who posed a threat to the President. It was said that if the OPP had been fully operational during earlier presidential terms, and Sadam Hussein had been targeted and eliminated, a war could have been averted.

The protective bubble closed tight around the President, who emerged victorious from his meeting with representatives of ATU (American Teachers Union) by far the nation's largest teacher unions. The President easily won their endorsement for his proposed education plan. He was happy and so were they. Union leaders could not believe their ears and he was already counting their votes for his upcoming reelection.

The President's plan called for new teachers to have a starting salary of over one-hundred thousand dollars a year with performance bonuses doubling that amount. The number of teachers would triple in three years and a four year college education would be tuition free for all US citizens. It was more than the ATU had ever hoped, more than they could dream and this President was able to push things through his party's Congress. It was a done deal, the cost would be enormous, however ATU had gotten what they wanted and the President got millions of votes, sticking taxpayers with another multi-trillion dollar tab.

The White House had just received its fresh coat of white paint, getting ready for the upcoming party circuit. New Ambassadors would be presenting their credentials to the new Commander-in-Chief. President Hussein walked outside under the portico on the way back to the Oval Office. Stretching his long legs, attached to a six foot five frame, he had a walk similar to a jog for shorter men.

Cerab Hussein had been swept into power having never proven himself capable of running anything other than a political campaign. Regardless of whatever the political big wigs thought about him, he was their President, at least for the next four years.

It had been a tough and brutal political campaign, but their Republican opponents never had a chance with their old warrior of a candidate from Wyoming. The mood of the country was crying for change and a breath of fresh air after a season of eight years of a dogged Presidency. The country was getting its wish.

The Director of the OPP slid next to the President and whispered something in his ear, causing the President to pause, then turn to face Director Cartwright.

"Why did the NSA call this meeting? And why all the mystery?" The OPP circle around the President widened out of hearing range as the two men had their private conversation.

"They received a private intercept going to Prince Rashid in Saudi Arabia and wanted to brief you on its contents."

"You see them and then come see me. You know how I hate seeing these bureaucrats. Take care of it," he spun around, continuing his morning jaunt leaving Director Cartwright standing in the light under the portico with morning glow beaming through the Jasmine and Wisteria trellis.

"Yes sir, Mr. President."

Benjamin Franklin Cartwright was a long time Secret Service operative and the mere mention of his name in the ranks of the Service spelled fear to anyone who knew him, or knew of his reputation. He was a tall, non-descript man of Ukrainian decent with a marine cut haircut who had spent twenty years in Special Black Operations in the CIA and FBI, before coming to the Secret Service. His personnel file was not available to anyone except the President, who appointed him to his current position after a four hour interview with the country's new leader.

Cartwright always dressed the same every day: black suit, black tie and white shirt, which soon became the unofficial uniform for those handpicked by Director Cartwright to join the OPP.

Cartwright was a tough cookie, captured by the North Koreans in a Black Ops gone bad. He was held and tortured daily for over three months without giving up so much as his name to his captors. He never spoke of the incident and the U.S. government never even acknowledged his existence until he was released, nearly dead, left adrift in a rowboat off the coast of North Korea. He was unable to walk for months after his release since the North Koreans broke both of his legs in multiple places.

The NSA driver pulled up to the White House gate and stopped to show credentials of himself and his two passengers, Director of the NSA, Jack Drury and his aide, Assistant Director, Commander Parker Johnston. They were waved through and met at the portico entrance by the President's Chief of Staff, Karl Wilson, a long time confidant of the President.

"Right this way gentleman," said Wilson as he led them down the hallway, through additional White House Security, then into a small elevator which sped upstairs towards the Oval Office. They emerged in a small anteroom of an office with no name or title on the door. It was strange in this town of one-upmanship not to have a sign on the door so near to the President, screaming one's significant.

"Have a seat gentleman. He will be right with you."

A few minutes later the door opened and they were greeted by a tall imposing man dressed in a sharply tailored Brooks Bothers suit, but still incapable of hiding the outline of his pistol under his left armpit.

"Good morning gentlemen," he said with a slight Eastern European accent. "I am Benjamin Cartwright, Director of The Office of Presidential Protection. Please follow me."

They followed Cartwright into a smaller waiting room through another security scanner until they reached a very non-descript office. The room was small, hosting a wooden desk and on its surface lay a pen and pencil set and a picture of the President with his family relaxing on the beach. There were no other pictures in the room nor could they see any of the usual framed diplomas on the wall.

"You have a document for me to see," he asked extending his hand.

"Yes sir, we have a document," replied Johnston, pausing, "for the President."

Cartwright still held out his hand and said, "Gentlemen let me be brief and to the point. The President is in the midst of some very lengthy and delicate negotiations, of which I am unable to expound on at this time. He asked me to meet with you gentlemen, assume responsibility for the document you have and deliver it to him, personally."

Johnston started to protest about how the Director of the NSA was being swatted away by a glorified bodyguard, until Drury settled his hand on his aide's arm to restrain him.

"Mr. Cartwright, we appreciate the time you have taken to see us," Drury interjected. "Please deliver this document to the President and should he want to be briefed further regarding our continuing analysis, we would be happy to return and provide additional input." With that Drury stood and shook Cartwright's hand and exited through the same door they came in.

"What was that all about?' asked Johnston of his longtime friend.

"We came to see the look on the President's face when we told him about the document but his refusal to see us told me what we needed to know. When we get back to the office set up a lunch meeting, very low key, with Jimmy Galloway, Assistant Director of the FBI. I think it's time we bring him into the loop and besides I haven't seen my old friend in over a month." It's time to talk to him. We need to talk about POTUS.

Chapter Eight

Nick Ryan woke the next morning with a huge hangover, his head cradled on his arm at his desk, his revolver still in his hand. He looked at it strangely before returning it to its rightful place in the lower desk drawer. His apartment was in shambles and he reeked of whiskey and cologne and old pizza boxes. He picked up his old six string guitar and began to lightly strum an old Chris Norman song, *Baby I miss you...*

Lifting his head, he saw the picture of him and Katie, as if she had never left his life. Her face, full of smiles, looked to be saying, *You have to make a decision. Do you want to live or do you want to die? No in between Nick, make up your mind. Do it now!* She always asked the tough questions.

It was time for him to get on with his life. He rose from the chair picked up the picture and after kissing it, he began his cleanup. That morning he filled three heavy duty contractor trash bags with whiskey bottles, newspapers, magazines, beer bottles and other assorted bachelor trash.

Nick went out on the deck and filled another large trash bag. It was remnants from what he had lying around and been accumulating over the months he was living there. He looked over to the other patio where he had last seen Rosa. It was empty. *Way to screw things up hotshot,* he told himself. When the place looked as normal as he could get it, he jumped in the shower, shaved, then headed to get a haircut. He'd made a decision: get on with his life, or at least what was left of it.

Coming back from the barber and Publix supermarket with two armfuls of groceries, Nick noticed a snappy black Porsche convertible pulling out of a parking spot three spaces down from him. It was Rosa. Taking a deep breath, he flagged her down.

"Good morning," she said with a slightly reserved smile, while stopping the car halfway out of the space.

"Good morning, Rosa, I wanted to apologize big time for my behavior last night. I was way out of line and owe you an apology."

"Apology accepted. I didn't mean to pry. I was only trying to help."

"Maybe we can try it again sometime, soon?"

"I would love that," she said, her smile warming her features. He noticed her short blue skirt hiked up as she kept her foot on the brake pedal of the speedy German sports car, once again revealing those gorgeous legs of hers.

"You know Nick, I should tell you that I was trying to help you through your grief yesterday, but I should also warn you that I find you wildly attractive. I had a special evening planned last night, with a bottle of French champagne on ice. Frank Sinatra on the stereo, I had a well laid out plan for last night to see where it would go. You really screwed that up."

Nick's face contorted in mock pain and he grimaced, to show he was sorry for messing up, then a smile returned to his face.

"Sorry, Rosa, can I have a rain check? Please?"

"Sure," she said her smile spreading across the rest of her face, her legs twitching to try to hold the growling Porsche in place. "How about tomorrow night, say seven? I'll cook up some Gnocchi and pesto, Chianti and we'll see what happens."

"Sound's great. I'll be there with bells on." He leaned inside and kissed her briefly on the lips. She started to blush.

"Now who is screwing things up?" he jested as she backed up the Porsche.

"Seven o'clock, sharp. Don't be late. Bye," she said over the sweet exhaust noise of the flat-six Porsche engine.

Nick hummed a tune as he bounded up the steps, two at a time towards his apartment. His message light was flashing and he turned it on as he put away his groceries.

"Hey Nick, old buddy, this is Jonathan. I need a favor." Jonathan Murray and Nick used to work together at the FBI, but then Jon and his wife started a family and he promised his wife he would be home more nights. He easily secured a job at Global Life Insurance as a Chief Investigator and Nick had helped him out of some jams in the past.

"I have a quick job for you if you can spare the time. I can pay the same compensation as before, plus expenses and a bonus, but I need it done right away. Call me when you get this message." *Beep.*

Nick dialed the number and the nervous claims adjustor answered his phone. "Special investigations, Jonathan Murray speaking."

"Jon, Nick Ryan. What's up?"

"Hey Nick, I have a large life insurance claim, five-million dollars that the police call inconclusive and my internal guys feel it's a suicide. I need a non-biased investigator to take a look at it. But I need it done real quick, like by tomorrow, otherwise it goes to arbitration on Monday and we do not want that to happen. Can you help me out?"

Nick grew silent as he mulled the offer over in his mind. The timeframe seemed awfully tight, he thought. He didn't want to be late or miss his dinner with Rosa.

"Nick? Nick are you there?"

"Yeah, I am here. I have dinner plans with a lady for tomorrow night; special plans and these quick one day things always seem to drag on. This my first date since Katie died."

"Nick, I'm sorry to ask you this but I am in a real jam," pleaded his friend. "It shouldn't take more than a couple of hours. It's pretty much an open and shut case of suicide. All I need you to do is go to the location, look around, talk to some neighbors and then fax or email me your report. You'll be home in time for your soiree dinner tomorrow night, I promise. It shouldn't take long at all. I really need your help. I have nowhere else to turn. I'm pleading with you. I would go but it's my kid's birthday and if I miss another one, I am a dead man with my family. Please Nick!"

"Are you sure I'll be done by tomorrow?"

"Of course Nick, it's a slam dunk. I'll have you home in plenty of time for your date."

"Okay, email me all the information."

"You're a lifesaver Nick. The file will be on its way within the hour and I'll have the plane tickets waiting for you at the airport."

"Where is the location, Jon?"

There was silence on the other end of the line.

"Jon, where am I going?" Nick repeated.

"Baltimore. You are going to Baltimore, Nick."

Nick took a deep breath, looking at the picture of him and Katie on his desk and replied, "Okay, Jon, get that info to me ASAP. I want to be in and out of there as quickly as possible and Jon, you owe me big time."

Nick left the next day on the first flight out. He had a three o'clock return flight and he would be home in plenty of time for his rendezvous with Rosa. His father wished him a safe journey knowing that Nick had not been back to Baltimore since his wife died. He glanced out the window of the plane and watched the clouds and landscape pass him by. The clouds all reminded him of things from his past. All of his memories of his life in Baltimore flashed before him, the good times and the dark memories. He remembered the last thing he asked Jonathan, "What is the name?"

"His name was Maheed, Hakim Maheed."

Chapter Nine

On one hand, Nick was excited about going back to Baltimore but on the other it was the place of haunting memories and served as a constant reminder of what he once had. His life had been perfect, now he just wanted to try to get on with it.

In some ways he wished he had time to stay longer—he would go see his "Uncle" Jimmy or maybe track down his oldest friend, Tripp Jackson. Tripp disappeared right after Katie's death and Nick had not heard from him, despite repeated phone messages.

He and Tripp had been college roommates, joined the Marine Corp and were stationed overseas together. They had both been involved in Black Ops missions on more than one occasion so it was only fitting that Tripp be his first choice for best man at his wedding.

Tripp and Katie hit it off immediately and Tripp used to joke that he wished he had been the stupid one to wear a Penn State t-shirt to a party where he and Tripp met Katie. But he had lost touch with Tripp, like the earth had swallowed him whole, without a trace.

His "Uncle" Jimmy wasn't really his uncle but was his mentor when he first joined the Bureau. Jim Galloway had taken him under his wing. He was a longtime friend of Nick's father and Jimmy had really helped him get through his rookie year at the FBI Academy.

Stepping off the plane he forgot how cool Baltimore was in early May compared to South Florida. The trees were starting to turn green after a hard winter, with the spring showers making everything smell so fresh. He did love springtime in Baltimore.

His heart raced when entering the BWI Airport terminal, half expecting to see his Katie waiting for him when he stepped off the plane, just like she always did. He was home, but the memories of home gripped his throat like a huge hand causing him to catch his breath. He could not breathe. *Nick, get control yourself.* He could no longer fight off the feeling that his Katie was still here. He knew he would need to confront his demons, sooner or later.

He read through the file on Hakim Maheed on the plane ride from Florida. It seemed like an open and shut case except for a few things that he kept going over and over in his head. Maheed had fallen off the balcony on the eighth floor of his condo building. He had left no note, which was not unusual in suicides. *Why would he commit suicide? Why had he raised his insurance policy by millions of dollars just prior to his death? Big changes to an insurance policy right before someone's death usually signaled a suicide.*

Nick would find out, file his report and be back in Florida for his dinner with Rosa. He did not want to spend any more time in Baltimore than was necessary. Although it would be nice to see Tripp and Uncle Jimmy while he was here, Baltimore had too many memories for him and besides he had spent months in Baltimore searching for Katie's killer to no avail.

Nick opened the file and read that Maheed was a Doctor who had worked before his death as a Senior Research Fellow at Johns Hopkins School of International and Arab Studies. He was also a top Bio-Hazard expert and also very well connected in the Arab community and spoke at least five languages.

Maheed traveled all over the world. How did he get the money to afford a five-million dollar life insurance policy? The premium on the insurance policy had to cost a fortune. The policy listed his daughter, Adriana Maheed, as the beneficiary.

He drove through the city in his rental car and continued up Charles Street until he was in the area around Johns Hopkins University. The school had bought hundreds of old buildings and converted them to student housing. Students filled the sidewalks, as they walked along the old tree shaded streets to classes and prepare for their final exams.

Nick continued to drive slowly until he found the place he was looking for, the Inn at the Colonnade, and pulled into their parking lot. It was a secluded building, containing a small boutique hotel on the first floor, a fine dining restaurant on the second and condos on the upper floors. It was popular with senior professors because it was within walking distance of the University.

Johns Hopkins University, Hospital and Applied Physics Lab was a sprawling complex, a huge organization in Baltimore, with over fifteen-hundred buildings in thirty-six locations. The hospital had an international reputation for quality and the Theoretical Applied Physics Lab (TAPL) attracted the finest minds in the world. Nick should know, his Katie had worked there.

Penn State and Johns Hopkins had been intercollegiate rivalries for decades. Katie had gone to Johns Hopkins and went to work at TAPL after she got her doctorate. There was always a bit of teasing going on anytime Penn State came to town and played Johns Hopkins. Nick made the mistake of wearing his Penn State t-shirt to a Hopkins party in Baltimore after being assigned to the local FBI branch.

This tiny little squirt of a woman, with oversized glasses, sandals, a sloppy Hopkins t-shirt approached him pointing a finger to his chest, poking him furiously and asked, "Are you that brave or that stupid? Huh? Are you?" He just smiled at her. She was so serious he could not get mad at her. He was also eight inches taller than her and the sight of this tiny PhD poking an oversized jock in the chest was laughable. But all he could do was smile and soon the anger left her lips and she broke down laughing. He and Katie were inseparable after that.

Everybody wondered what the attraction was, she the brainy Physicist at TAPL and Nick the jock FBI agent and incurable romantic from Penn State. But it worked. They were soul mates. He got along well with her friends at work, Natalie, Joshua and Samantha, but especially well with Natalie. Nick could not help but smile thinking back to that first day.

He took the elevator up to the eighth floor of The Colonnade and used the pass key from the front desk manager to let himself in. The room was quiet, the drapes pulled back. Books and stacks of paper, lined the wall and the floor soaking up the silence, demanding more in return. He walked around the apartment before walking out onto the balcony. Nick could see most of downtown from this small balcony including the school and some nearby restaurants, banks and shops.

He knelt down to examine the floor and the banister and observed nothing to indicate a struggle, no scratches, no usual scuff marks associated with a fight, nothing. He examined the sliding glass door and saw no grab marks anywhere, which you usually found if there was a clash.

The banister was installed according to HUD Senior Standards, meaning it was eight inches higher than what you usually found in an apartment building, impossible to accidentally fall over. Maheed's death was no accident, that Ryan knew for certain. Ryan saw no sign of a struggle and nothing that would indicate a conclusion of anything other than a suicide.

He took over twenty photos of the balcony and surrounding businesses below. Convinced of his preliminary decision, Nick returned inside. He observed the entire living room, like a photographer, one frame at a time and took more photos. He walked around and tried to get a feel for the room. It had been searched and searched recently. The searcher was good but had made some mistakes. Someone had taken all of the books down from the shelves and looked through them one by one. *What was the searcher looking for?*

When the searcher, whoever he was, returned the books, he had returned them hurriedly, as not all of them were facing the same way. The dust marks on the shelf were inconsistent with where the books were now situated. Someone had moved them all and replaced them, but not to their original location.

Nick's detective mind slowly began churning, his eyes taking it all in. On Maheed's desk was a month at a glance with last month's calendar replaced by a fresh, empty month, nothing written on it.

He sat in the dead man's chair and looked at the phone and some of his personal belongings. Hakim had a genuine Turkish puzzle ring hung over his pen and pencil set. The only place to find one like that, was in Turkey.

Legend has it puzzle rings were originally used as wedding rings in Turkey. There was a secret as to how the four intricate pieces of the ring fit together which was only taught to Turkish men. If the wife took the ring off to be unfaithful, the ring would come apart and the husband would immediately know of her transgressions. The smart wives merely went to the Bazaar themselves and purchased multiple rings for themselves paying a pricey premium.

Since this ring was silver, it was meant for tourists and usually purchased in the Grand Bazaar in Istanbul. A small strand of wire held the multi-piece ring in place, so it would not fall apart, so it had not been worn yet. Nick surmised it was recent a purchase because the silver tourist rings did not stay together too long after being purchased.

On Maheed's desk were two pictures, one of him and a young woman, with the Eiffel Tower in the background. The way he was hugging her told him she obviously was not family. The other photo Nick picked up and he examined, while leaning back in the chair. He guessed it was taken at a lake rather than the ocean because of a Chris Craft motorboat moored behind them. Hakim held up a trophy fish, a lake trout. The photo was taken by a stranger or set on automatic, since it was slightly off center.

In the second picture, Hakim was standing and laughing with another woman, possibly family, because of her resemblance to him in the picture, perhaps a daughter or a niece. She was very pretty, tall compared to Maheed standing next to her, thin, with long black hair and an intriguing smile. She was a real beauty, the kind of beauty that sends nations to war. This had to be the daughter, Adriana.

How could he get in touch with Adriana? Maybe Jonathan at Global Insurance had her number—he'd have to if she was the beneficiary. Nick pulled out his cell, about to dial when the door to the apartment swung open. It was her—standing right before him.

"Who are you?" she bellowed, walking towards the desk. "And what are you doing behind my father's desk? Well?"

"My name is Nick Ryan." She was even more beautiful in person—her deep dark eyes, now filled with anger and mistrust, were captivating.

"My name is Adriana Maheed. Hakim Maheed was my father. What are you doing here?"

"I was hired by Global Insurance Company to investigate your father's death. They want me to determine if it was a suicide or not and they need someone from outside the company to provide an objective investigation."

"Why are you sitting down at my father's desk? If you are here to investigate then investigate. Do you have an ID or something?"

"I have my FBI Identification if that will do? What do you think caused your father's death? Do you think it was a suicide?"

"No, I don't. My father lived his life to its fullest and we were getting ready to travel together to South America, just the two of us. We were going to visit a friend in Buenos Aires. I don't think he would take his own life two days before my arrival. Do you?"

Looking at her blazing dark eyes, filled with a mysterious eastern passion, he would have to agree with her. *The last thing I would want to do is to kill myself if this raven haired beauty was coming into town to see me.*

"I don't know but a lot of what I see here doesn't add up. Did your father have a cell phone?"

"Yes, he had a Smartphone. He always had it with him. He used it for messages, texting, for note taking and had everything organized in it. I could not imagine him without it."

"Did the police give it to you?"

"No. I had not even thought about it until you mentioned it."

"I didn't find it here. What was the phone number?"

"I called his cell number last week a couple of times and just get a message that it was out of the service area."

"Call the number again, using my cell phone," he asked her. The same phone company message was broadcasted. Puzzling? He walked around the old man's desk taking it all in, as if he was memorizing it for review later. Nick retrieved a photo from the desk and asked, "When was this taken?"

"Last summer."

"Where was it taken?"

"My father has a lake cabin in the mountains at Deep Creek Lake out in Western Maryland."

Showing her the other picture he asked her, "And who is this?"

"That's his little friend, Clarisse, in Paris. They met two years ago. My father tells me everything including all about his girlfriends. He was faithful to my mother while she was alive, so I cannot deny him his female companions. All men have needs."

Nick looked at her.

"What needs do you have Nick? Are you a gambler? Women? Do you like the drink? Or something stronger?" She was testing him.

• • •

Nick stood up and took one last look around and snapped some photos for the file and then returned to the balcony. He took out his pocket telescope and scoured the surrounding cityscape and then took some more photos from the balcony.

Nick ignored her questions and told her, "Well, it was good to meet you, Adriana." He hated to leave this dark haired beauty but he had to get on with his report and return to Florida.

She blocked his path and her sweet flower-like perfume filled his senses as her eyes captivated his soul. Those eyes now riveted into his, she asked him, "So what will your report say, Mr. Ryan?"

"It will say that it was a suicide rather than an accident because the balcony is just way too high for someone to fall over. It is eight inches higher than your normal every day balcony and it is made just for that purpose, so people don't fall off their balconies and die."

She gasped slightly when he said this to her.

"Adriana, for someone to get over the top of this banister he would have to have jumped or been pushed by someone. It is too high of a banister for someone to fall accidentally. And since there was no evidence of anyone else being here, it looks to me to be a suicide. I'm sorry, but that's what my report will say." Nick felt a twinge of guilt for not being able to tell her what she wanted to hear.

"That's what the insurance company was saying before you got here. It sounds like you agree with them. Mr. Ryan, I know my father did not commit suicide. I know it but I need you to help me prove it. Is there anything else you can do?" she asked with her imploring, piercing deep eyes which were surrounded by the darkest eyebrows and lashes he had ever seen. They lured him, held him, and twisted him. She moved closer to him, her breasts just barely touching his chest, tantalizing him.

Nick was torn. *So much for a quick visit and back in time for dinner with Rosa, these quick trips always lasted longer than he thought. He should have known better than to listen to Jonathan. He was resigned to the fact he was going to have to stay at least one more day to do his job right.*

"Tell you what, join me for dinner tonight."

She gave him an odd look and backed away. "I am not looking to buy a favorable report. I am just trying to get to the truth of what happened to my father. I loved him dearly and the only way I could get an investigator assigned to my father's case was to file a claim with the insurance company. I don't care about the money. My father provided very well for me. But Mr. Ryan, you are my last hope."

"Listen Adriana, I know all about not knowing about how a loved one died can tear at the fiber of your being." He stopped. "Meet me for dinner tonight at the Hyatt downtown. I have some other things I want to look into. I will be able to tell you then what the final report will look like. Is that fair enough?"

"Fair enough," she said as she backed away and they both left the apartment.

Walking down the corridor of her father's condo building they passed apartment 802, with a black wreath on the door.

"Did someone die there?"

"Yes, a friend of my fathers. It was a home invasion gone terribly wrong. It was a couple of days after my father's death. Someone ransacked the apartment and brutally murdered him."

"What was his name?"

"His name was Joseph Santino. He used to watch my father's apartment while he was away. You know, water the plants, watch for mail and packages, stuff like that." Once on the street Nick drove around the neighborhood surrounding the Colonnade.

He was tortured about what he was about to do until finally he called Rosa. He called three times and on the third try he left a message for her saying how bad he felt about canceling dinner with her. He had been looking forward to it and hated canceling. He would have to figure out some way to make it up to her. He did not want to stay here, Baltimore had so many memories and demons for him to face. But maybe now was the time to start.

Over the next four hours Nick made more than ten stops until he found exactly what he was looking for, pay dirt. He headed downtown to check in at the Hyatt, the same hotel where Adriana was staying. Now he had to buy some clothes, a toothbrush and a razor.

Heading downtown on the Jones Falls Expressway he found he'd picked up a tail as he left the Colonnade building, a four-door dark sedan trailed his every move. *They were professionals.*

Chapter Ten

Senator Abe Speigelman looked at his watch impatiently while waiting for his lunch companion, Assistant Vice-Attaché for Agricultural Affairs at the Israeli Embassy, Ari Ben Rubi. The small restaurant *Andiamos* in Georgetown was popular with the International set but too far to go for most busy congressmen. The place just reeked of money and Abe Speigelman felt right at home.

He was a four term Senator from New York and headed up some of the most powerful committees on the Hill. No one ever expected a kid from Brooklyn, being raised in the garment business with his father and uncle, to rise to the pinnacles of power in Washington.

Senator Abe Speigelman understood one thing from growing up in New York, money is power and lots of money is lots of power. As he prospered in the rag business he made a lot of wealthy contacts in the Jewish business community and soon became one of their biggest fundraisers for Jewish causes, charities, Israel Bond fund drives and political parties that looked favorably upon the preservation of Israel. He'd been to Israel many times and the government there made him an honorary citizen. When he retired, he decided he was going to move there with his family. It felt like home.

Abe sipped his martini and watched his dining companion walk through the busy eatery to join him in the rear of the restaurant where they could have a private conversation. The big Israeli walked like he was in no hurry but his keen eye did not miss a single detail as he sat down in the booth next to the congressman. The bench seat dipped slightly under the weight of the newest occupant.

Ari Ben Rubi had the sometimes impressive, title of Assistant Vice-Attaché for Agricultural Affairs at the Israeli Embassy in

Washington. In reality he was a key player in Washington for Israel's Secret Intelligence Organization, the Mossad.

"*Shalom*, Abe," Ben Rubi said, greeting his old friend and his country's strongest supporter in Congress. Ari Ben Rubi had been in the Mossad for over thirty years. His older brother was one of the Israeli athletes killed at the Munich Olympic massacres and he was determined that something like that would never, ever happen again.

After he completed his mandatory military service he applied to join the Mossad. Ben Rubi was turned down as being too much of a hothead. Over the years he kept applying until they accepted him, just to get him out of their hair and they tired of saying no to the persistent young man. It was the best choice that either one had ever made, for he became an invaluable asset to Israel and the Mossad over the years.

"*Shalom*, Ari. *Mah Ha'Inyanim?*"

"Everything is good. The usual and no matter what Israel does, we are always in the wrong. It never changes but we must always be vigilant."

"Yes. I know."

"What is going on with this new President? On the one hand, every Israeli program that your congress has funded including black operations, aid and education, everything, even aid to Israel defense is being cut by this President. We don't understand. On the other hand, he is spending this country to ruin but he won't help the only democracy in the Middle East, his only supporter and ally."

Ben Rubi reached for the bread basket and began tearing the warm rolls into pieces, trying to fit the large portions into his mouth.

"I know, I know. He is a difficult one to understand," replied the concerned Congressman. "But when he spends more money on internal matters here at home there is just not enough to go around to our allies, including Israel, Britain and our defense alliances such as NATO." The waiter brought more bread and handed them the menus as he read off the daily specials. After they ordered their meal

Ben Rubi waited for the waiter to retreat before going over the reason he asked for the meeting.

"I did not come here today to complain but to bring you up to date on some troubling matters. There is an undercurrent of some activity taking place globally that we have not been able to piece all together yet, but it involves the solvency of this country and it is trying to undermine your governments support for Israel. The Mossad has been tracking a package that left the Middle East and was shipped to the United States. Your country's NSA and CIA is finding out bits and pieces of what was in the package. We do know that anyone who came in touch with it is dead. Our info is sketchy at best but it now seems that the FBI is also involved."

The young waiter brought them their lunch as they made small talk before resuming their conversation.

"Ari I need more information. Much more! I need names and dates. Is this nuclear? Biological? Financial? I can't do anything with the information you have given me. It is way too sketchy." The Congressman became concerned because the big Israeli sitting across from him was not usually an alarmist. "Do I need to make contacts and bring in the CIA for a sit-down? Do I need to request a meeting with the President? What do you suggest? I can do very little with the information you have given me so far."

"Be patient, old friend. We are still looking into it but you know as an Agricultural Minister my role has to be circumspect at best. I will keep you informed, I promise. I must go to brief the Ambassador. *Shalom*, good friend. *Kol Tuv*." After wishing him well, the Mossad agent stood.

"*Shalom*, Ari. See you soon." Then as an afterthought the congressman added, "Ari, have you found any oil yet?"

"No we haven't, but we keep looking just like we have been for the last twenty-five years. It is tough because none of the Multinationals will drill for us. I guess they are afraid of pissing off the Saudis."

"I know, but there is little we can do about that, God knows I have tried to persuade them, dragging them up to Capitol Hill. But I'll keep trying."

The big man looked at the Congressman and said, "Abe, the only name I have for you is, Hakim Maheed. He lived in Baltimore."

The big man stuffed two dinner rolls in his suit pocket for later and waved goodbye. He was joined by two men in ill fitting suits who had been sitting near the front entrance of the restaurant and the group of them made their way into the warm May afternoon sunshine in Washington, DC.

Abe Speigelman had lost his appetite and left for once without ordering dessert. He needed to make some phone calls. Dialing the number in his cell phone, he quickly connected to his contact at the FBI, "Assistant Director, James Galloway, please, Senator Speigelman calling."

Chapter Eleven

John Nagle woke up and turned over on the old beat up sofa inside his field office trailer, which he now called home. The big Texan spied the large stack of unopened bills sitting on his desk, next to the mound of the ones he had opened weeks ago, all unpaid. He was alone in the trailer which now also doubled as his home since his house was foreclosed on twelve months ago.

Nagle lost his home, his car, his boat, the beach house in the islands, and the company's office building, but what hurt him most was losing his loving wife Estelle eighteen months ago to cancer. This all happened in the past two years, it was the worst time of his life.

He'd bet and bet big, as most oil wildcatters do, on his dream of finding the big one, the one big field to call his own. Today he had his final meeting with the remaining members of his board and his banker, William Newton from First Texas Bank.

Nagle traveled all day, the day before, to come back from overseas and his drilling site deep in the gulf, off the coast of Israel. He had gotten into Houston late the night before and crashed at his new home, the trailer in the equipment yard. He'd slept in worse places but today he could not remember where nor did he really care, It was over. Today the bankers were going taking away his baby, his one remaining joy in life, his company, Nagle Oil Exploration.

All his banker needed was for his board to vote on the bankruptcy filing. There was nothing he could do to stop them, he had spent everything he had, everything he could borrow and leverage, trying to find oil or gas off the coast of Israel for the last six years. He mortgaged his house, his company and any other asset he could use to keep his dream alive. Most of his board backed him, maybe not backing his dream but backed him, John Nagle, they believed in *him*.

Most of his board, who had been with him since the beginning of the company, would lose most of everything they had as well today. They'd financed the company until the very end. But John Nagle was different, at age sixty-six he was too old to start over, to go to work for a major oil company and help them find oil. He just could not do it. The problem was Nagle Oil was really the only job he ever knew.

Nagle Oil, first started by his father back in the sixties, was considered large by wildcatter standards but new finds had to come every year in order to survive. His father taught him everything but the one thing that he did not teach him, something that was innate with the younger Nagle was, he had a nose for oil. He could smell it and over the past twenty years his nose had been more right than wrong. Now Nagle was seeing the end of an era, the end was fast approaching for this wildcatter and his company. All he had to do was sign the papers.

He walked to the back of the trailer, shaved, brushed his teeth, opened an old wooden tool cabinet that served as a clothes rack and sniffed under the arms of the white shirts hanging there looking for the cleanest or least offensive smelling shirt he could find. When he was satisfied, he tied on his lucky green Irish tie and headed for his old rusted Ford pickup truck to make the trip to downtown Houston.

The drive to his former headquarters in Houston was bittersweet and took him over an hour, but gave him time to think. His downfall had been what he thought was one of the most promising sites he had ever seen. The geologicals looked great, the test drillings were promising and even though the target site was in the same area as the large Tamar basin, all his test wells came up dry drilling in two-thousand feet of water.

When he first went to the site, accompanied by a representative of the Israeli Petroleum Agency, he had them stop the boat and drift. He could smell the oil in the air, he could taste the natural gas in every fiber of his being, his hair stood on edge, it was electric but it proved elusive and he never found anything to justify the continued drilling expense. Now it was all over.

Production would be shut down at the drilling site at noon today, just when he was to sign the final bankruptcy papers of the once legendary Nagle Oil and Exploration Corporation of Texas. He was resigned to that fact, but he still felt there were billions of barrels of oil underneath that deep dark water in the Mediterranean. He just would not be the one to find it. He was out of time.

He pulled into the parking garage of the tall office building, containing over twenty floors of glass and steel, which was formerly the headquarters of Nagel Oil and now the executive office building for First Texas Bank. His banker had snatched up John Nagle's old corner office and had the nerve to schedule his final meeting with Nagle in his old boardroom. He got a salute from the longtime parking attendant, Shelley Karls, "Morning, Commander. Great to see you again, sir. "

"Hi, Shelley. How's Melissa and the kids?"

"Just fine sir, thank you for asking. Take that end spot there, the one marked reserved. Mr. Wilson won't mind. Besides my last day is Friday. They let me go after fifteen years with the company. Cost cutting hogwash. Anyway, it's just not the same without you here, sir."

"Thanks, Shelley. I appreciate your support. Are you going to be looking for a job? I can put in a good word for you and ask around if you like."

"Mighty nice of you, sir. I appreciate it. You're a damn good man. Have a good day and give 'em hell, sir."

Scores of people stopped Nagle in the hallway and the elevators, as he made his way to the top floor. The board was assembled around the former Nagle Oil conference table waiting for him.

His longtime partner, Trenton McCartney, handed him a Bourbon and Branch saying, "Drink up and spit 'em in the eye, Johnny."

"Trent, you know I don't drink when I'm working."

"Hell, this ain't work, this is going to be a celebration. We are going to finish here, go out and get drunk and tomorrow we start a new company. We'll grab a couple of rigs and find us some oil, hell we're in Texas, where you dig a vegetable garden and you find oil, lots of oil."

"I'm afraid it's not going to work that way anymore, Trent. Our time has come and gone now it's time for us to move on. I'm going to miss all of you guys. You been with me through the thick and the thin, now it's over. Cheers!" The room broke out in laughter and bravado.

The celebration was soon cut short by the arrival of a tall, skinny suited man with tortoise shell glasses that appeared too small for his face. His three piece suit was perfectly tailored for him, as long as he did not gain an ounce of weight. His squeaky, irritating voice sounded as if he were wearing underwear that was far too tight. It was William Newton, Nagle's banker.

Newton held out his hand to his longtime client. "Good morning Mr. Nagle, John. Good to see you. Sorry I'm late. Someone parked in my spot in the garage and I had to park on the street while they towed the old truck away."

Nagle grimaced but held his tongue.

"Good to see you, Will. You have good taste in offices," said John Nagle.

"Thank you John," he said, at first not realizing that Nagle had dinged him again. *That would soon be over and so would Nagle Oil Corporation. Gone. Finished. Done. Out of his hair. He no longer would have to deal with this old, upstart businessman that dealt his own cards and played by his own rules. Now the roles were reversed and John Nagle would sign his own death certificate,* thought Newton smugly.

"You know that this hurts me as much as it does you, John. I have a lot of money invested in this company. I will miss you."

"Listen here, Billy boy, you don't have any money invested in this company, you little twerp," he said, finally being pushed over the edge by this young pipsqueak, who went right from college to the bank his father founded. "You have other people's money invested here. Everybody from your bank that has lent this company money has been paid in full." He paused to look around the room at his old friends, then continued, "The men in this room, on the other hand, have money invested in Nagle Oil and they are the ones that I feel for, not you. So don't tell me you have money invested here, because you don't."

"John, I think it's time to sign the papers, don't you? Then we can all go about our daily business. If that's all right with you?"

"Yeah, let's get it over with, tell me where to sign."

"Let me get the papers from my secretary, Margaret. You remember Margaret don't you, John?"

"I should, she worked for me for over twenty years. Damn fine assistant. Better hold on to her."

"Ass," said the room in unison, when the banker left to find the paperwork for the last meeting of Nagle Oil.

"Any word from Clark, Johnny?" asked Trent, referring to Nagle Oil's top field driller on site in the Med.

"No. I feel like the condemned man waiting for the governor to call and give a stay of execution," said Nagle. "They are supposed to keep drilling until noon, then the funding runs out. Don't expect the Governor to call, old friend, it's over. Time to move on."

"Here we go gents. Here is a copy for everyone," said Wilson returning to the conference room with the documents. "John, I just need your John Hancock on this line right here. Then all of your misery will be over. Sign here."

"Before I do, I want to take just a moment to thank everyone here in this room for all of your support over the years. You believed in me when no one else would and I tell you today I will, never, ever forget it. Thanks, you are the best friends a man can have."

"John, please, sign here. I have other matters that I must…"

There was a knock on the glass wall and John Nagle could see his longtime aide, Margaret Thompson rushing towards the room. "Sir, there's a call for you, sir," she said poking her head in the conference room.

"Thank you Margaret? What line?"

"The call is on line six Mr. Newton, but the call is for Mr. Nagle." Nagle smiled and rose from his seat to take the call. Wilson did a slow burn but he knew this would soon be over and he could get on with his day.

"Commander? Hi, this is Clark Wooden. You are not going to believe this, sir, but you were right, you were right all along! Shit, I can't believe it myself and I'm here. Can you hear that rumble in the background? Can you hear the roar of gas and oil cursing your name, you son-of-a-bitch? We struck the biggest mother-load in history, right where you said it was going to be. Goddamn! I'm in love and this love is so damn intoxicating. Get your ass out of that smelly suit and get back here where you belong…, sir."

"Holy shit, Clark! Let me put you on speaker phone, the whole board is here, along with our banker. Tell them what you just told me."

"Gents, hi this is Clark, Clark Wooden, Drilling Superintendent on Leviathan off the coast of Israel. We struck the largest load of Natural Gas ever found, anywhere. And Nagle Oil is sitting right on top of it."

"How much gas Clark?" The room was all ears, grabbing the rest of the Bourbon and sending young Will Newton out for more.

"It is still clicking Commander but we passed ten trillion cubic feet five minutes ago and it is still clicking. I can't believe it. Have a drink for me, sir and I will see you when you get here."

"Did you say trillion?"

"Yes, sir and it is still clicking. Oh my god, we just hit twelve trillion! Shit!"

"I'll be on the next flight out, Clark. Good work."

"Yes, sir. You have made the small state of Israel not only totally self-sufficient in oil and gas for the next one hundred years but now it is an oil exporter on the scale to rival Saudi Arabia. And get this, the country of Israel doesn't even exist to the Saudis. Ha-ha-ha. So sweet. See you soon sir."

Will Newton entered a room overcome with celebration and set down two bottles of Bourbon on the table with a bucket filled with ice. "Congratulations John," he said as he quietly tore up the bankruptcy documents and shoved them into his pocket. "I guess we'll be talking about a new line of credit for NOE, right?"

"Right you are, Newton. Except this time I am going to a different bank, one that can shoot straight with their customers. And be loyal. See ya soon and don't get to comfortable in my corner office there Willy boy. I'm going to want it back real soon. Bye men, I'm back to Israel. See ya later."

The very next day, John Nagle bought some new jeans, shirts, work boots and boarded a flight to London. He was a very happy but troubled man. Nagle had to make sure that his WP lease rigging deal was still rock solid, otherwise it would all be for nothing. He needed those drilling rigs from WP now more than ever.

Chapter Twelve

Downtown Baltimore had experienced a renaissance of building construction bringing in the National Aquarium, a Science Center and the crown jewel on the inner harbor, Harbor Place, a shopping mecca filled with fine shops, wonderful restaurants and lots of tourists. The other jewel, rising fourteen floors above the Inner Harbor, was the Hyatt Regency hotel towering over the magnificent downtown revival.

Ryan's room on the seventh floor at the Hyatt had a wonderful view of the harbor including that of Fort McHenry and the gleaming National Aquarium. He watched the sailboats gliding through the water, with sails tipping to the breeze as they raced the wind and soon all the memories came rushing back to him.

It brought back memories of water taxi rides with Katie in the Inner Harbor, going from one restaurant to another. They would take a boat ride and start with the Rusty Scupper for fresh homemade crab soup, climb back on the water taxi and head south to the Bay Cafe for seafood and then to Fells Point for dessert, homemade coconut ice cream, and finish up at the Aquarium and the Fells Point nightlife area for a nightcap. He thought of her infectious laugh and smiled to himself.

Nick grabbed a shower, changed clothes and headed to the hotel restaurant called *Fishers*, on the fourteenth floor to meet Adriana for dinner. He had just sat down when he saw her walking towards him. He watched Adriana's slow and deliberate walk and noticed the men at the bar stare at her in idle pleasure.

She forced a smile as she sat down, not knowing what to expect from Nick's report. She ordered a glass of wine and looked closely at Nick. "Well, hello again." Her gaze avoided the manila folder lying in front of him on the table. "Nick, whatever you found out and regardless of the final report, I want to thank you for everything you did. I appreciate your checking further for me. It is awful having someone you love die and not know why."

He moved the file to the side and looked at her dark eyes which were focused on him.

"Adriana, there is something I must tell you. My wife was brutally murdered over a year ago and to this day I do not know why." Nick was not used to talking about his personal feelings with anyone except maybe his father but for some reason he wanted her to trust him. He wanted to let her know that he understood more than anyone what she was going through. "I loved her and not a day goes by that I don't miss her, so I can appreciate exactly what you are going through right now." He paused while the waiter, dressed in a white shirt, black tie and red vest with splatters of the evenings' pasta menu speckled on his uniform, brought them their drinks.

"Beautiful view, is it not? You have the best table in the house," interjected the brash young waiter before he retreated back to the kitchen.

Nick continued to tell this strange new friend his deepest feelings, why he did not know other than he too could feel the pain that she was experiencing.

"Adriana, I have tried to get on with my life and everyone tells me it is time to let it go but it is hard, very hard. The hardest part is admitting to myself that I don't know what happened or why it happened."

He leaned back in his chair and could see the sailboats in the Inner Harbor below, racing to get into dock before the sun set. He opened the file and she moved closer to him with the faintest scent of her sweet perfume wafting in the air.

"Adriana, from the balcony of your father's apartment I could see a lot of shops nearby and in the blocks surrounding his condo. I went and visited them after you left. I reviewed pictures from their security cameras and had them make copies for me."

He laid out ten photos on the table. Some pictures were clearer than others. "I believe that is your father."

The picture from the bank's surveillance camera showed a man dressed in blue on her father's balcony. Time elapsed photos showed him falling. Tears welled in her eyes as she looked at the picture of her father falling to her death. She began to cry.

Nick closed the folder Nick, "We can do this at another time if you like."

"No, no, tell me everything you know, everything."

He showed her all of the photos, holding back just one.

"Your father was not alone on the balcony." He showed her a picture of her father and a set of hands and arms pushing or chasing him.

"Your father's death was not a suicide, Adriana. He was pushed."

She gasped. "I knew it! I knew my father would not take his own life."

Nick pulled out some pages he received from the phone company. "I also had a log trace on your father's phone done by a contact of mine at the phone company and I have a list of everyone he had called over a two week period leading up to his death." He showed her the list of local and international calls that her father made.

"These are a lot of numbers. What are you going to do with this list?"

"I am going to contact them and see if I can find out what connection there might be, if any, to your father's death. I'll let you know what I find out."

"No," she said adamantly. "I am going with you. I can help you."

"No, I don't think that is a good idea. I don't know what I am going to find."

"You are going to find out what happened to my father."

"No, Adriana, it is too dangerous."

She took the list from his hand and pulled out her cell phone and began dialing one of the numbers at random. From all of the numbers she dialed he knew it was an international call. He could hear the phone ringing and a man answered.

She handed the phone to Nick and said, "Here, you talk to the man, you do speak Arabic don't you? French? Farsi? I didn't think so."

She retrieved the phone from Nick. The man on the other end of the conversation continued, *"Salam? Salam? Hello?"*

"Salam," responded Adriana sweetly.

"Kadar? Chi shod?" What's wrong?

"Esm e shoma chist." Adriana asked for the man's name.

The man on the other end of the line hung up quickly.

"We need to call him back and find out who he is and what his relationship is to my father."

"Later," responded Nick. "We may need more help than we thought."

She smiled as she perused the list, "Nick, I speak seven languages fluently and three others good enough to get by just like my father. Americans can say hello and goodbye in high school Spanish or French and think they can speak the language. Nick please let me help you." She leaned into him, the scent of her perfume was intoxicating and he could the feel of the warmth of her body which compelled him to agree. *Maybe she could be of help.*

"Okay, we start first thing tomorrow. We start by calling these numbers on this list and see what we can find out. Can you get us into your father's office at the University?"

"Sure. I know the people there and they have been calling asking me to clean out his office so they can reassign it to someone else. That should be no problem." She laid her hand on his and smiled. "Thank you Nick."

He walked her to her room. "Goodnight. Sleep well; you are going to need it."

She placed her hand at the back of his neck and pulled him closer, so close he could see the depth of her deep dark eyes. She kissed him. Gently at first, then more passionately she pulled him close until they were touching. He could feel her chest against his, he breathed deep. Suddenly his arms were around her. She made him feel alive again. She kissed him once more, deeper.

"Goodnight Adriana," he said, still catching his breath, pulling back. "We have a long day ahead of us tomorrow." He felt guilty to Katie's memory and for some unknown reason he felt he was betraying Rosa, whom he had just met. His emotions were so twisted.

Chapter Thirteen

A soft voice whispered his name in an old familiar tone. "Nick… Nick." It was his Katie.

"Hello, my love," he said. "I've missed you."

"I know, but I'm here now. I'm always here for you, baby." She smiled that twinkling smile of hers and walked towards him.

A horn blasted its annoyance on the street below, waking Nick in a sweat drenched frenzy. Nick jumped to his feet and turned on the light. She was gone.

He'd slept fitfully as usual and walked over the window, to watch the deserted Baltimore streets below. Everyone was home in bed. He tried to sleep but kept waking. The green hued face of the clock radio on the bedside table reminded Nick it was two a.m. Early morning rain pelted the glass with its own rhythm and style.

He dressed and took the elevator to the garage and soon traveled up Interstate-83. It was raining heavier and the car's wipers worked furiously to clear the rain from the windshield of his rental car. His drive was random at first but soon developed a purpose. He drove towards the beltway and cut over the side roads and soon he was driving North on Harford Road.

Baltimore's Harford Road started downtown in the city with two lanes running past old neglected mansions long past their glory days of Baltimore in the 1930's. The street ran for blocks until it widened into six lanes of congested traffic shooting straight through the heart of the city until it reached the suburbs.

The road narrowed to four lanes before dwindling to two lanes when it meandered into the countryside outside of the Baltimore. Soon it was a windy, tree lined narrow country road making its way past the horse farms in the outer suburbs of the lush green Maryland hills and valleys.

The rain increased in intensity. Windblown leaves made the curving road even more treacherous and slippery. He passed over the wide watershed with its ornate bridge and tall iron structure arching over him with the fast moving waters racing below. Still heading north he looked for the entranceway to his driveway off to the right. Homes became sat further off the road and less visible along the way, sitting further back away from the twisty drives shrouded by overgrown trees.

His heart pounded when he saw the stone chimney jutting high over the trees around the bend in the road and knew he would soon be home. He pulled the rental car into the driveway, slowing down as a car passed him. The house looked the same and he thought he saw Katie standing inside, waiting for him.

The house was a restored, one bedroom old stone manor house, overlooking a small stream which sometimes became a raging river during heavy spring rains. But during the summer they would make homemade *Limoncello* and let the bottle chill in the cool streaming water below.

He stayed in the car staring, the wipers making the house he and Katie renovated for two years visible every couple of seconds.

Leaves collected at the base of the French front doors and the windows were covered with dirt and everyday traffic grime.

The rain let up some and he made dash for the front door, reaching over the stone mantle and searching for the key with his fingers. His outstretched fingers found them just where he'd left them. He picked up the accumulation of circulars and phone books at the base of the front door and walked inside. The house was exactly as he left it. The furniture was still covered with ghostly white sheets and the stone floor clicked hard under his heels. This was home, this was his heart. He stood there, in silence.

The small house contained one large room on the first floor with a two story cathedral ceiling making it appear much larger. The stairs at the far wall, led up to the bedroom he and Katie had shared. Nick walked with heavy feet up the short stairway, until he stood there looking at their bed, with time not a consideration, it seemed like yesterday. He stared, memories came rushing back, pushing him. He marveled the bed was still there, since Katie was gone so should the bed, strange logic he thought to himself.

Her clothes were still in the closet. Nick pulled them close to him and buried his face, luxuriating in the comfort of her being there with him. The sweet lingering perfume filled his nostrils. He could smell her, feel her, so close. He thought of her. God did he miss her. He pushed the clothes back before trudging downstairs, not really knowing why he was there.

He saw the outline of Katie's computer sitting on her desk with a towel draped over the top, covering it. He touched it, her constant companion for years and it was like touching her. He flipped it open, touched a button and it sprang to life, shocked it still worked after all this time. He caressed it. It brought back memories of watching her toiling at her desk for hours. He missed her. His heart ached from missing her. He missed her touch, he missed her laugh, he missed making love to her.

Slumping into her chair, he reached under the drawer retrieving the cold hard steel revolver he secured there. It looked strange in his hand. He spun the chamber and placed it to his head, click. A second time he pulled the trigger, click. He waited for a moment, his head dropped. He pulled the trigger a third time, click. He pulled the trigger back slowly before releasing it and began to cry. It was the first time he had cried for her.

She was gone. He replaced the cold steel revolver to its resting place under her desk drawer. He folded his arms and slept at her desk, missing his Katie in this place they shared, this place they called home.

"Nick? Nick darling." It was Katie's voice. He looked at her, so close, so full of life, with her twinkling green eyes and that sparkling smile. "Nick I came to say goodbye. Don't follow me, please."

"No Katie, I couldn't bear it if you left me again. You left me before. Please don't go, please." She kissed him on the cheek, he froze and could not move.

"I will see you soon enough. I must go now. Goodbye, my love," she told him lingering just long enough for him to capture her face for eternity. The front door blew open, a gust of wind sheared by him and she was gone. She wasn't coming back.

That was the last he remembered. He fell asleep in her arms and dreamed of her with his head lying on the hard wooden desktop.

A van driving by stopped in front of the house, and shined a flashlight on the front door peering inside, looking and watching.

Chapter Fourteen

They burst into the small cabin and rudely woke Nick from his tortured sleep at her computer. He could see the shadows moving fast, talking Russian, all dressed in black with masks covering their faces. There were at least six of them. Nick jumped to his feet, and as the first one reached for him, Nick delivered a strong punch to his stomach, then round-kicked the second one to his side and made for the pistol under the desk drawer.

He was shoved backwards onto the floor by the tallest one and then pinned down by three of them, the strong smell of vodka slapping his face. Nick flipped one, kneed a second and rabbit punched the third assailant. He again tried to reach the desk but suddenly jerked back, falling limp to the floor in a fit of convulsions as they zapped him with six-million volts from a stun gun. He faded into unconsciousness, his body felt frozen.

Nick Ryan awoke from his ordeal lying in the back of a van speeding over rough, dirt roads and every time it hit a pothole or bump he could feel something wrapped around his neck, choking him. He had a rough burlap bag over his head, tied at the neck, smelling of week old fish.

He heard Russian voices and laughter. He went to move and a boot shoved his hip.

"*Ne peremeshchaite.*" The man gruffly told him in Russian not to move and then pushed him again with his boot. Nick's hands were tied behind his back, tight. His feet were bound with wire going from his feet to his neck, where it was pulled tight. Any movement on his part brought choking and excruciating pain to his throat. He lay still and tried to collect his thoughts.

The van smelled of burlap, sulfur and gunpowder. He surmised it was an assault vehicle where they made their own ammunition. The floor of the van smelled of fresh paint. He did not know how long he had been out nor how long they had been traveling until the van abruptly stopped, bringing fresh pain to Ryan's neck. The van honked and the sounds of a garage door, probably a large commercial door of some type, slowly creaked open. The van lurched forward and stopped with screech.

The door of the van slid open and he heard more Russian and Albanian voices. Two men grabbed him roughly and hustled him out of the van before throwing him on the ground. His air was abruptly cut off by the tight wire wrapped around his throat.

He felt the familiar presence of a boot on his hip, it was a firm boot sole, probably a reinforced paratrooper boot. He could smell the salty ocean air mixed with the strong presence of diesel fuel. *This has to be a marina or boatyard of some sort.*

Nick felt the wire around his feet being cut and then the one connecting his feet to his neck also cut. Relief, finally he could breathe freely again. He gasped for fresh air.

He was pulled roughly off the concrete floor and thrown onto a metal chair with his hands still tied behind his back and the burlap bag still over his head. He could sense the men around him, walking in a circle.

Steps approached him and stopped. Then his hands were moved and the plastic tie was cut, releasing them. He rubbed his wrists to regain blood flow to his numb fingers and hands. He waited, ready for anything.

He sat and heard nothing. He felt hands lifting the burlap bag and the light blinded him. As his eyes adjusted to the spotlights aimed right at him, he saw his tormentor, face to face. It was his old friend Tripp Jackson.

"Hey cowboy, you are getting slow in your old age. How the hell are you?" said Jackson, handing him a beer.

"TJ, you son-of-a-bitch! What the hell are you doing? You scared the shit out of me."

"Sorry old friend but we are doing field rendition drills posing as Russians to throw off any blame if it goes wrong. I wanted to bring you in and get together with you and felt you were a great target to practice on. If my team could get you they could get anyone."

A big African American, a huge linebacker football sized team member, walked over and slapped Nick's back. "Didn't mean to rough you up there partner, but the Chief said to bring you any way we could. Hell, you need to thank him, my team wanted to strip you bare and really make it authentic but the Chief here said no way. No hard feelings, right?"

"Right," responded Nick.

"Let's go over here to Cent-Com and let me brief you. Man is it good to see you. How the hell you been holding up?" Tripp said.

"Good, I guess."

"Bullshit. You can't fool me. We both miss her. I kick myself every time I think about it. She was the best. She was that rare combination, funny, bright and downright gorgeous. But you need to keep your wits about you. You are walking into a hornets' nest and you don't know anything about it. I had to pull you out of harm's way to let you know what's going on. Dig?"

"Yeah. By the way where the hell you been man? I have been trying to get in touch with you for months," Nick said to his longtime friend.

Tripp appeared tired but looked to be probably in the best physical shape Nick had ever seen him. His hair was cut Jarhead short and his t-shirt was stretched tight across his chest with his ever present cigarette pack stuck underneath his left t-shirt sleeve. He smiled and then Nick knew that it was the same old Tripp.

"I've been in Black Ops exclusively old friend for the last year, just like the old days. Only this time we trained for a much longer time. I volunteered for the mission over two years ago and we are just now getting done with it. We went in with six Rapid Assault

Team Packs low over the border, with four Black Hawks and two large Sikorskys. We had four reserve helos on the ready just in case our target was wounded and we had to bring him in or anything else that could have happened. But if he made one move we were told to blast him, they didn't want him blowing up the whole place with our teams along with him, just like he always said he would do."

"Wait Tripp, are you saying you went in after Krazir?"

"Yeah, man. We got the old son-of-a-bitch. When we were finished with him we grabbed up computers, laptops, flash drives, notebooks, diaries, calendars, everything we could carry and made a survey of the place. The Pakis must have heard the bullets and all because we were alerted that a Pakis military convoy was heading towards Krazir's house. We grabbed everything we could and got the hell out of there."

"No shit?"

"No shit. Yeah man, it was a real rush. I'm only sorry we had to lose one of those sweet choppers. Well, the Pakis were royally pissed and kicked a lot of the guys from the Company out of the country. They told us never to come back."

"You working for the CIA now Tripp?"

"Yeah, old friend, always have been, since the beginning, even in the Marines. Sorry, I never told you. They wanted it that way."

"Really?"

"Yeah, man. Well, we get a call from the kind folks at Inter-Service Intelligence Directorate / Pakistani Intelligence asking us if we want to come back to Abbottabad and pick up some sensitive equipment from the downed Black Hawk and invite us in to search and survey the old coots house.

"The Pakis didn't have the equipment like we do and they were looking for something, what we didn't know but they wanted it bad. They also said they would turn over some of the truckloads of stuff they hauled away. So back we go with all of our gear, including infrared cameras, particle detectors, x-ray equipment and everything else we could bring, then we went stomping through the compound for five days."

"We took clothing samples, DNA samples, and then we x-rayed the entire house. We finally found a safe hidden behind a wall and the Pakis wanted us to x-ray it. It contained *beaucoup* cash; I mean a lot of cash. That's what they wanted, they took it and then we never saw them again. We brought in all of our specialists with us. Nick, you look thirsty. You want another beer?"

"Yeah, sure Tripp." The beer was going down real smooth, thought Nick, rubbing his sore throat as Tripp continued his story.

"On the last day we found a hidden room behind a false wall panel. We thought it might be a panic room but it turned out to be a storage place where we found loads of data files. I mean *beaucoup* files and papers. In a secret floor panel we uncovered a box with Biohazard—Level 3 emblems all over it. Now we know that Krazir was into anything he could use to kill Americans so we are really careful with this one."

"Great beer and great story but what does it have to do with me?"

"I'm getting to that part, just wait." Jackson took a long swig from his cold beer. "It was the size of a shoe box but it was lead-lined and we could not see inside with our x-ray gear and it was locked on the outside. So we're not taking any chances to try to blow it or try to unlock it. We gave it to our Bio-Hazards specialist, a longtime agency guy with links to the other side and then we head back to base alpha for a further examination. He decided he wanted to bring it to the lab at Langley. So off he goes and that was the last we ever saw of him."

"Yeah and…?"

"The guy turns up dead a week later."

"Yeah and…? Who was he?"

"His name was, Hakim Maheed. The guy's death you have been looking into. His daughter is gorgeous by the way. We have been looking for it ever since but so have the Saudis, the Russians, the FBI, the Paki's and everybody else. Have you come across it?"

Nick was floored. What had he stumbled into? "No, sorry to say I haven't seen it."

"Call me ASAP if you do. And whatever you do, don't try to open it. It could be booby trapped."

"What's in it?"

"Beats the hell out of me. It could be the Bubonic Plague for all I know. We don't know because we never got the chance to look inside. But what we do know is that Krazir was a crafty fox and it could have been anything from a biological weapon to some secret papers that he really did not want anyone in the world to see."

"That's the best you can do?"

"Nick it could be his little black book with the names of all his hookers around the globe for that matter. I would not put it past him. But I tell you one thing, everybody and their sister wants to get their hands on it. Also, you got a tail on you that is hot for it."

"Who's the tail?"

"I don't know, I think it's private. You want me to take care of 'em?"

"No. I'll be all right."

"Okay, just watch your back, good buddy. We are still checking it out. Come on, your car is outside and you can head back to the hotel. Here's a number you can reach me at twenty-four-seven. Now you see why I could not get in touch with you while all of this was going on? It was a total communications clamp down. We'll get together soon, just in the meantime watch your back. Okay?"

"Yeah, yeah. What does this box look like and do you think it's still around?"

"We don't know for sure but we think it is highly unlikely. Our strike team is out of it now and the real spooks from all over the globe are looking for it."

"Got to go now old friend, call me if you need me. There's your car. And Nick, one last thing, you should know that the guy who handled the call log search for you at the phone company, Ralph Miller, died two hours after you called him for the numbers you needed. He had a blow dryer fall into his tub at home and was electrocuted. I don't believe in coincidences. Let me know if there is anything I can do."

"Well, there is something you could do to help, old buddy," Nick said and reached into his pocket, handing Jackson a copy of the log sheet. "Let me know anything you can about the people on this list, ASAP."

"Okay, I'll see what I can do."

Nick left the old industrial warehouse section near the Inner harbor of Baltimore and driving back to his hotel, his mind raced a mile a minute trying to digest everything Tripp told him. Where was all of this leading? It was supposed to be a simple suicide investigation.

He drove up I-395, past the old piers and waterfronts long deserted, past the old fish trawlers listing to one side, tied precariously to an abandoned pier.

Now he was involved with the beautiful and mysterious Adriana. He had to trust her and now he had to find the metal sized shoe box. His answers would be inside.

Nick drove by the old oil terminals, which sat all in a row, waiting to be refilled, badly in need of a fresh coat of paint as the brown rust crept up their sides. He took the next exit and headed towards the hotel. *Time to get some rest. He had a big day ahead of him.*

Chapter Fifteen

"Good morning, Mr. President."

"Tell me how your meeting went," the President responded with obvious irritation, dispensing with all formalities and niceties as he walked around the Oval Office. He continued to look out the window at the tourist busses parading down the street past the White House.

"Fine, sir," said the security officer, handing the NSA folder stamped *Top Secret* to the President. "They wanted you to see this text message that was sent from Maheed's apartment in Baltimore to Prince Rashid in Saudi Arabia by Rashid's son Yasim. Apparently, according to my sources, the FBI is also now involved. One of their investigators, Special Agent Nicholas Ryan, has been investigating the death of Mr. Maheed."

The President's eyes drilled into his top security officer. "At whose direction?"

"We don't know yet, sir. I know Nick Ryan, I worked with him and his father. He is a good investigator, hangs on like a bulldog. According to his file, he apparently is on a temporary administrative leave from the Bureau and not on the active employee roster. He had a nervous breakdown after his wife was found murdered about sixteen months ago and went on a wild goose chase to locate her killer. He is also very tight with Jimmy Galloway and his father retired from the Bureau a while back on disability leave."

"This is getting out of hand," the President responded. "We must rein in this operation before anything else happens. I would like to meet with Mr. Ryan. Please arrange it, as casually as possible. Do you understand?"

"Yes, sir, Mr. President. I know exactly what you mean, sir. Will there be anything else, sir?"

"No. Close the door on your way out." The President told his secretary that he was not to be interrupted and walked around the Oval Office before stopping in front of the full length mirror situated on the side wall. Pressing the corner panel, it swung open and he proceeded up the previously hidden steps. The lights were activated by motion sensors, guiding his steps.

The desk at the top of the stairs was his from his Senatorial days and the laptop was one of the few possessions he brought with him to the White House. The system started up immediately and he clicked on the internet browser searching for AlifMusic.net. He downloaded the first three and the last two selections and spent the next two hours listening to the instructive voices of Prince Rashid and the commands of Al Jezzera. It was his way of relaxing and communicating. He had his instructions. He knew now what he had to do.

Chapter Sixteen

Nick and Adriana climbed into the Chevy and pointed the rental car up Charles Street towards her father's office. The traffic became heavier as they reached the visitor's parking lot surrounding the huge University. A security guard patrolling the lot walked towards them but stopped, assured that they were not interloping students looking for a free space.

Nick was tired from his meeting with Tripp the night before. Rushing back to the hotel, he showered, changed clothes and went to meet Adriana for breakfast. He thought about going home and sleeping in his and Katie's bed but it was beyond him now to sleep there without her, he could not do it, at least not now. He needed more time.

They walked through the common areas of the University with the sounds of foreign languages floating in the air, some that even Adriana was unfamiliar with despite her vast linguistic abilities. Johns Hopkins University attracted students from all over the globe to study, to dream and contribute to the world of knowledge at large.

They reached the International Fellowship Building and Adriana led the way to the third floor and unlocked her father's office with a key he'd given her. The office was much like his home with clutter everywhere, piles of papers, leaflets, flash drives, books all stacked neatly around the room and lining the walls. Nick did not tell Adriana about his meeting with Tripp and their search for the missing shoe box of great importance.

The office bookcases were overflowing with papers and books some half opened, lying on his desk. The desktop was no exception to the apparent disorderly array of materials that he kept. There were mountains of paper everywhere.

Nick walked around the room, tip-toeing through the narrow pathway between stacks of books and reference materials intermingled among boxes and boxes of papers, stacked in some unknown order, known only to the late Dr. Maheed. He was a true researcher who threw nothing away.

Nick settled in at the desk and ascertained that this room had also been thoroughly searched. On the desk was a picture of Maheed and his daughter and another picture of Adriana and of a woman who had to be her mother. The resemblance was unmistakable.

"Your mother?"

"Yes. It was taken on my tenth birthday. Do you see a family resemblance?"

"Yes, you are both beautiful," Nick said without even thinking about what he was saying.

Adriana blushed. "Thank you. What are we looking for here anyway?"

"Some indication as to what your father was working on here." Nick continued to survey the room for any clues but found the same thorough search procedure had already been applied to this room as Maheed's condo. *It was clean. He would find nothing here but took some pictures anyway. A picture did not lie and would not forget.*

"Let's go, Adriana. I think we are done here."

They walked past the same security guard that they'd seen coming in but now Nick's car was surrounded by a group of eight black XL Suburban SUVs. Nick knew those vehicles well from his short time on the Presidential detail when the President went overseas and his local office in Moscow provided backup support for the Secret Service.

"Ryan, Nick Ryan?"

Nick looked at the tall Agent walking towards him. It was OPP Director Cartwright.

"If this isn't a coincidence I don't know what is. How the hell are you?"

"Good, Ben. How have you been?" Nick never believed in coincidences, especially when it came to Cartwright.

"How's your Dad, Nick?"

"He's good. Thanks for asking."

Ben Cartwright had a fierce some reputation outside of the OPP. He was someone you did not want to cross, but for some reason he and Nick seemed to hit it off. Maybe because Nick's dad was old school FBI and Cartwright was one of the few old timers who would appreciate father and son both in the same agency. Nick liked him, always did.

"How's the OPP?"

"The same, life never changes, just a new President every four or eight years."

"I'm sorry, Ben, let me introduce you to Adriana Maheed. Her father was the late Doctor Hakim Maheed, he was a professor here at Johns Hopkins. He died a couple of weeks ago in his apartment at the Colonnade. What are you doing here?"

"I am here doing some preliminary ground work for the President's speech to the Johns Hopkins graduating class in three weeks."

"Well, it was good to see you again, Ben. We got places to go and people to see, if you know what I mean." Nick turned towards the car.

"You know Nick," Cartwright said, motioning for him to wait, "we had tried to reach you earlier in Florida and they said you were traveling and unavailable. The President is hosting a black tie dinner to honor your mentor and old friend Jim Galloway. He wanted to invite you to the Kennedy Center for the affair. I know it is short notice but if you are available I am sure both the President and Mr. Galloway would welcome your presence. What do you say?"

Nick turned to face Cartwright. "Well, I am only in town for such a short time and I doubt you would have time to perform your famous OPP clearance on me in time."

"That is not a problem, I will rush it through. Besides you are a FBI Special Agent and a guest of the President."

"I don't have a tuxedo. I was only supposed to be here for a couple of hours and head back home to Florida."

"We will contact the Hyatt and arrange for them to send up some tuxedos to your room to choose from. And if there are no further obstacles I'll bid you good day and look forward to seeing you tonight."

"There is just one other small problem."

"Yes? And that is…?"

"I don't have a date, unless Ms. Maheed is available to attend with me tonight?"

"I would love too, Nick. Thank you so much for asking," replied the smiling Adriana.

Cartwright was flustered and momentarily out of words. "I suppose if you vouch for her, then we can have her attend as your sponsored guest."

"Wonderful. Thank the President for the invitation and we will see you tonight."

Driving back Adriana said, "What a turn of events. A presidential dinner, a formal affair. Who would have thought, you know, running into him there? What are the chances of accidentally running into him? What a coincidence."

Nick did not say anything but he knew otherwise and he certainly did not believe in coincidences, especially where Benjamin Cartwright was involved. The OPP knew he was here all along, otherwise how did they know he was staying at the Hyatt? *Coincidence my ass. But why?*

Nick waited for Adriana in the lobby of the hotel that night, fitted with a tuxedo that was too long in the legs and too snug around his broad shoulders. He ordered a limousine to pick them up at the hotel and take them to Washington, DC. It would be worth the money.

Ryan forgot about all of his discomforts when he saw her riding down the escalator to meet him. She looked breathtaking in her shimmering dress, midnight blue to highlight her deep and intriguing eyes which were partially covered by her traditional veil. The sheer veil was trimmed in hand woven silver threads and her eyes came shining through. She was spellbinding.

Nick now understood why Middle Eastern men went wild for women in veils, it inspired and heightened the imagination. Adriana's dress however, departed from the traditional garb, in that it had a slit which ran high on the side of her leg, stopping way above her knee showing her most beautiful legs.

"Good evening, Nick. Is something wrong?"

"Yes, you look criminally ravishing and should be locked up."

"Don't make me blush, Nick."

He reached over and sought her hand, cradling it gently in his, squeezing it while he softly touched her fingers.

She looked at him, smiled. "Don't start something you can't finish, Nick," she said. Now it was Nick's turn to grin and blush.

Chapter Seventeen

"Welcome to the United States, Mr. Richards," said the middle-aged female immigration official at Dulles International Airport greeting passengers disembarking from the Air France flight from Paris. She looked up from Jasara's forged passport photo to match it with the face in front of her. The British forgery was quite good, the best in fact since he bought it from a contact who worked at the British Passport Office in London.

"Thank you. I am looking forward to my stay here," said Jasara well dressed in the navy three-piece suit and burgundy tie with matching silk square protruding from his suit pocket.

"Business or pleasure, sir?"

"Business unfortunately. I am here to attend the International Symposium on Government Relations, being given by your government at the Commerce Department. Hopefully, I will be able to sneak away for a couple of hours and see some of the sights."

"Your first visit to the U.S.?" she queried him while she scanned his passport through the Passport Security Profile System.

"Yes, it is."

"Well, you are in luck," she responded, handing him back his passport once the green light lit up on her computer screen. "The cherry blossoms are in full bloom this week."

"You don't say. I have heard wonderful things about your cherry blossom festivities. That settles it, I must get away to see them. Thank you for mentioning that to me."

"Have a nice visit, Mr. Richards and welcome to the United States."

Jasara hailed a taxi from the waiting line and settled into the back seat of the yellow car. The cab had a strange musty smell lingering in the air at the rear. In his travels he had smelled worse but rolled own the rear window a crack to breathe some fresh air. He watched all the people bustling by. He always liked visiting the United States, the people here had so much and did not even know it.

"Where to bud?" asked the Pakistani driver, holy beads hanging from the rearview mirror.

"Take me to the Grande Hotel please."

Jasara set his black briefcase on his lap and popped it open. He reached behind the rear flap and pressed the bottom which opened a hidden panel and quickly changed his passport and identity. He pulled out a Canadian passport and some cash from the stack of bills found there. The cab pulled in front of the grandest hotel of all, The Grande. At least the grandest and most favorite of Jasara of all the hotels he visited in his worldwide travels.

"Welcome to the Grande, Mr. Wilson. Is this your first time staying with us?" queried the petite young woman at the registration counter.

"No, I have been here many times. Miss, I have had a long flight and I would like to ask that I please not be disturbed for the rest of today, if I may. I desperately need some rest."

"Of course, sir. Your room is ready now. Would you like to order room service, orange juice, coffee, croissant or something, sir?"

"Thank you, but the only thing I would like now is some sleep."

"Of course, Mr. Wilson. I hope you enjoy your stay here with us at The Grande. If there is anything we can do to make your stay here more pleasurable, please do not hesitate to let us know."

"Thank you."

Jasara tipped the bellman carrying his bags and immediately positioned the smaller, tan one on the bed. He unzipped the luggage and felt the bottom of the pull handle for a small button and pressed it. The handle disengaged and he reached inside to pull out a small piece of green putty-like material wrapped in plastic. He cautiously unwrapped the sticky material on the bed and placed it in a small metal container. He went to the stairwell, walking down fifteen flights of the hotel's rear steps to the street below.

Jasara hailed a cab. "Take me to the corner of Pennsylvania and Tenth, to the restaurant *John Michel*."

"Ah good choice, very nice restaurant. You will sincerely enjoy, sir," the cab driver said with a decidedly strong foreign accent.

This time of day the restaurant was not busy and Jasara chose a table overlooking Tenth Street. He ordered a light lunch, with the Moroccan coffee he loved and waited.

From his seat by the window Jasara watched the busy Capital bustle by in cars, limos and people, lots of people. Some were government workers in ties and many were tourists in shorts with their ever present camera dangling from their necks. He saw executives in dark suits wearing shiny black shoes, walking and reading newspapers at the same time, not even looking where they were going. People talking on the ubiquitous cell phone as they hustled between offices and eateries, trying to maximize their lunch break.

Then he saw what he was waiting for, a young man, in his early twenties, obviously mid-eastern, in a white waiter's uniform, walk into the restaurant toward the rear to the restroom. The young man walked past Jasara without looking and five minutes later he left the same way. He proceeded outside without looking back and soon disappeared into the crowd.

Jasara paid his lunch bill and visited the same restroom, locking it behind him. He reached under the sink and felt until his hand reached what he was looking for and set it on the countertop. He retrieved the small green packet from his jacket and fitted the piece inside and replaced the item back where he had found it. It was picked up ten minutes later by the same waiter who left it in the bathroom. Jasara returned to The Grande, retrieved one piece of his luggage, walked down the steps and hailed another cab.

"Where to, sir?"

"The Watergate Hotel, please."

Jasara reached inside his jacket and pulled out a second passport, legal but stolen. The rightful owner of this Canadian passport, was the well respected Dr. Rodney Storm, who at that very moment was enjoying a vacation in Western Canada, fly fishing. Jasara's room at the Watergate Hotel overlooked the Saudi Embassy complex on one side and a front row seat with a clear view of the John F. Kennedy Center for the Performing Arts on the other side. It was a clear view, a straight shot so to speak. He laid down to rest, now all he had to do was to wait. He was very patient and very good at waiting. He looked at his watch, it was now only a matter of time.

Chapter Eighteen

American Airlines flight #535 from Houston arrived in Baltimore nearly forty-five minutes late, much to the chagrin of all of the weary travelers who had experienced the long flight. Carlos Scarlatti retrieved his luggage from the luggage turnstile, happy that his assignments were nearing an end. He had two more hits to perform and then he could go home. Home to his island house on Saint Thomas, home to his boat, home to his beach cottage and his Maria.

Thinking of all of that, he was distracted. He did not see the portly man, in the green, plaid sports coat, pass him in the terminal, turn around and, almost say his name. Instead Tito Ascenello, followed him to the downtown city taxi line, where he saw Carlos jump ahead of the line and was off, heading toward the city.

Tito, the accountant to the mob boss Marti Romano, had to let his boss know who he'd seen. He was sure it was Carlos Scarlatti. His boss, was right, *everything comes to he who waits,* and Romano had been waiting for years to exact his revenge, on his former fancy looking hit man. Tito could hardly believe his luck. Neither could Romano.

Carlos headed downtown and checked into the Hyatt Hotel on the revitalized city waterfront. He checked out the room and searched the hallway until he found the stairs, just in case he needed an exit route to make a quick getaway. He called the front desk and asked them to arrange for him to pick up a rental car.

This hit should be a snap. Soon he'd be on his way to his last hit in Washington D.C. and he'd be done. Then he could finally head home. The multiple hits had proved to be more tiring than he originally thought. He would be glad when it was all over.

Carlos made some phone calls and was angry at himself that he would have to spend one more night in Baltimore. His target was away camping at places unknown, somewhere in the Maryland boondocks and would not be back until the following day. His camping vacation gave this geek one more day to live.

He drove through the downtown waterfront area, posing as a well heeled tourist out for an evening of fun at the city's waterfront crown jewel, Harbor Place. Musicians strolled along the walkways and jugglers performed on the sidewalks, reminding him of the old city of Quebec.

Carlos made his way to the Little Italy section of town and was happy to discover the multiple choices of great Italian food available in such a small area. Couples walked hand and hand while families rushed to secure their seat at the nearby outdoor cinema where they showed great old film classics. Carlos laughed when he drove by and saw tonight they were featuring his favorite, *The Godfather*.

He parked the car on a side street and walked the short distance to the quaint little Italian restaurants. Some were very large, with outdoor tables crowding the sidewalks, like La Strada, overflowing with tourists. Other, smaller restaurants, some no larger than an undersized storefront, like Giada's, specialized in Sicilian cuisine and catered to the locals who lived in the area.

Strains of the mandolin floated in the air, notes of Al Martino, Tony Bennet and Frank Sinatra punctuated the festive atmosphere as he strolled the small crowded streets.

There were six to eight restaurants on every street in this small, six block area. Carlos perused all the menus as he passed by, not succumbing to the exhortations coming from the owners outside or the owner's sons, to come and try a meal at their wonderful restaurant.

Scarlatti settled on the Italian bellman's suggestion, *Buongiorno's* on High Street. He was not disappointed; it was superb, like being back in a New York restaurant. The restaurant occupied a former bakery with tiny mosaics of black and white tile usually found in a bakery still remaining, covering the spotlessly clean floor.

The waitress, with blonde and reddish hair piled high on her head, made him feel more like he was in a diner rather than a down home Italian restaurant, until they delivered his meal.

The *Caprese* salad with fresh mozzarella cheese, beefsteak tomatoes, covered in basil leaves and drenched in sweetened balsamic reduction was to die for and the homemade pesto and linguine melted in his mouth. The fresh ricotta and goat cheese *Cannoli* was so rich, he had to force himself to finish.

Pushing himself away from the table, he ordered a small glass of Limoncello but he could feel the eyes of some of the patrons watching him, looking at him, and he soon became uncomfortable. They were looking at him, talking to each other with their hands covering their mouths. Had he been recognized? His natural paranoia was running wild but that was always his fear, fear of being recognized. Time to leave and quench his other big appetite.

Carlos headed towards the strip joints and bars on the notorious Block, a short distance away. He found the comfort he was looking for, and paid to stay the night. Tomorrow was another day.

Chapter Nineteen

Nick could not take his eyes off of his date for the evening. Adriana was beautiful tonight and he was sure they would cause quite a stir at the Kennedy Center. Looking at the buildings speeding by as they made their way into downtown D.C., he turned to face her. She smiled that smile of hers, half knowing and half wondering.

"Tonight, we are just going to have a nice evening and enjoy the event," he told her.

"Yes, it should be lovely. I have never been to an event like this before. I did not have the time to shop for a new dress so I wore this. I wore it to a friend's wedding a couple of months ago. It was a very traditional wedding at that, all women were veiled. I had to stitch up the side slit for the wedding but for tonight I opened it, I hope you don't mind?"

"No, not at all. I find the veil around your eyes to be quite alluring actually."

"Are you flirting with me again Nick Ryan?"

"Yes, as a matter of fact I am."

"Good, I just wanted to make sure we were both on the same page. Maybe you can stop back at my room for some coffee or a nightcap?"

"I thought that alcohol was forbidden in your faith."

"It is, but I am not a real orthodox follower and besides who said anything about alcohol?"

"You said a nightcap, right?"

"Yes, I did, but where I come from that means something totally different."

"What does a nightcap mean where you come from?" asked Nick, grinning.

"You'll see tonight, my friend." Her eyes twinkled under her veil.

Nick was surprised that OPP would allow them both into this kind of event at such a late date. Usually the screening process for this type of affair, where the President was in attendance, would take weeks to accomplish. Nick closed his eyes. That was it, the President wanted him there. That was the only reason he had been invited. If it had not been Uncle Jimmy's celebration it would have been something else. That's what he had thought all along, but why?

What could the President of the United States possibly want from him, Nick Ryan a lowly FBI Special Agent?

He would find out soon enough, as the limo came to a stop at the entrance of the Kennedy Center. It was a spectacular building, the most lavish in all of Washington.

The impressive building was the brainchild of President John F. Kennedy, who was a strong patron of the arts. Fundraising had started shortly after he was elected but really kicked into high gear two months after Kennedy's assassination and ground was broken two years later. It took six years to complete the huge marble and glass tribute to the arts and to the nation. Kennedy had often referred to the arts as "our contribution to the human spirit."

The Kennedy Center was one of Katie's favorite places for the ballet, the opera and the symphony and they would make the hour long trek from Baltimore to D.C. Seeing the Center that night brought back many sweet memories to Nick.

The driver opened the door for him and Nick extended his hand to Adriana to help her out. Her hand was warm and soft. He looked down at it holding his, clutching her fingers gently. "Game time," he said under his breath. She smiled.

They both endured three security checkpoints, including the last one with the OPP. Cartwright was standing there in the background, observing everything and he managed a forced smile and short hand gesture to Nick, obviously not pleased with Adriana's attire. *Screw him*, thought Nick, *this is a free country, this is my free country*.

They made their way through the crowds and found their assigned table. He personally did not know anyone there that evening but the room was filled with familiar faces of Congressmen, lobbyists, movie stars and the like. Adriana took it all in, like a school girl going to the Academy Awards and seeing all of the famous actors and actresses. After all of the introductions at the table were completed, Adriana relaxed and had the time of her life.

"What would you like?" Nick asked her.

"I would like this to last forever, but I will settle for a glass of Chardonnay, thank you."

"Wine?" Nick responded quizzically.

"Yes, that's usually what a Chardonnay is, wine."

"I know what a Chardonnay is, I didn't think you drank wine, that's all."

"There are a lot of things you will find out about me tonight, Nick."

"Okay, I'll be right back. Will you be all right here by yourself?"

"Positively."

The event was a roast for his old friend and mentor, Assistant Director of the FBI, Jimmy Galloway. Nick could see Jimmy on the stage and got halfway there to greet him when the announcement was made for everyone to take their seats. Everybody took their turns telling their "Jimmy" stories, including OPP Director Ben Cartwright. It was a very nice evening and for once, Jimmy looked like he enjoyed being the center of attention.

When coffee and dessert were served, Nick glanced up to see Ben Cartwright making his way to Nick's table. Nick stood to greet him. The tall man stepped aside to reveal that President Hussein was following directly behind him.

"Mr. Ryan, such a pleasure to see you again," said the President, extending his hand to Nick.

"Mr. President, it is an honor."

"Nick, we met once before in Moscow. You were providing FBI security support to the OPP on my visit there. I never forget a face."

Nick remembered it well. He was working liaison with the Russian security detail at the airport and the Russians, looking to flex some of their international muscle, refused to give a takeoff time for the President's departure. Nick and Tripp went to the air traffic controller of Moscow's Sheremetyevo Airport and told them they were taking off at exactly at nine p.m. and if they did not want an international incident they would clear the airspace for the president's departure.

Later, on Air Force One, the President walked past Nick in the security area and tapped him on the shoulder saying, "Nice job Ryan," said the president, shaking his hand. "That's what I like, initiative." And then he strolled past, wearing his brown leather bedroom slippers. That was the last time Nick had ever spoken to him.

"And who is this young lady, Agent Ryan?"

"Mr. President, allow me to introduce you to, Ms. Adriana Maheed."

"*Salam,* Ms. Maheed. I was so distressed to hear about your father's death. Please accept my deepest condolences. His passing is a great loss."

"Thank you, Mr. President."

"Ms. Maheed, will you excuse us for a moment? I need to speak with Agent Ryan for few minutes. You don't mind if I steal your handsome escort away, do you?"

"Of course not, Mr. President."

"Ryan," the President began, as they walked away from the table with the tall man draping his arm around the shoulder of the young FBI Agent. "I am so glad that I ran into you this evening." They walked away from the table surrounded by the ever-present OPP protection bubble.

"It is so appropriate, you being here tonight honoring the great Jimmy Galloway. But you know and I know, Jimmy would surely agree, that our senior leadership ranks are getting older and they won't be around forever. His boss, Director Hickok, is too ill to even get off his sick bed and attend the festivities this evening."

The President paused to let his words sink in before continuing, "We have been starting to fast track key individuals to move up very quickly in our intelligence organizations, such as the FBI, CIA and NSA and others. I would like you, once you are off of your temporary leave, to join us in that endeavor, with an immediate promotion to Section Chief here in D.C. That is one step below Galloway's current position. What do you say, Mr. Ryan?"

"Mr. President, I am honored to be considered for such a program. I would like to ask for some time to think about your offer, sir."

"Sure. But don't take too much time Mr. Ryan, the world we live in does not stop turning. It is a dangerous world out there. Think about it and get back in touch with me, soon. You know where I live," he said jokingly. "Good night, Mr. Ryan."

"Good night, Mr. President. Thank you, sir." When Nick returned to the table, his mind was racing.

"Wow, some date you turned out to be. I am really impressed with your circle of friends," said Adriana when Nick sat down at the table. "You looked like you were old time friends with the President. What did he want, if you are at liberty to share it with me?"

Nick whispered in her ear, "You know the old saying, *keep your friends close but your enemies closer.* Well, he wanted me closer, that's all."

She looked at him quizzically before responding, "Well, I'm going to the ladies room. I'll be right back. Don't go away. I want to hear all of the gory details."

He watched her walk away and decided he was starting to have feelings for this woman. He felt a tap on his shoulder and looked up to see the huge cherub Irish face of his old time friend, Jimmy Galloway.

"Hey Jimmy! Sir."

"Sir? Cut the crap. You been here for two hours and I have to come down here to find you. I thought I taught you better than that. By the way who's the good looking gal?"

"That's Adriana Maheed, my date for the evening."

"Nice. Very nice. I'm glad to see you are out dating again. Maybe we can even entice you to come back to work?"

"Soon, Uncle Jimmy, soon," responded Nick to his father-like mentor.

"Nick, we need to talk privately. Let's go outside, so I can have a smoke. I have been dying all evening to have a cigar."

"Well, you got that right, dying is what will happen if you keep smoking those old stogies." Nick followed Jimmy to the terrace.

"Cut it out, you sound like my Mildred. She has been trying for the last twenty years to get me to quit. Hey, how's your Dad?"

"He's good sir. Still in rehab, but has some nice looking nurses taking care of him."

"How are you doing, son?" asked the older man, lighting up his cigar while surveying the sparkling city lights of D.C. all around them.

"Good, I guess, sir. As well as can be expected. You know what they say, one day at a time."

"You know I loved that Katie like my own, she made me smile that little spitfire, but I do have to say my eyes lit up when I saw you out with a date. And a pretty one at that. You always were lucky with the women."

His grin turned to a frown, as he leaned in close to Ryan. "Your name has come up on three different occasions over the past twenty-four hours, my young friend."

"Is that so? Who might I ask was asking about me?"

"Senator Speigelman paid me a visit and asked about you, then I got a surprise call from Jack Drury over at NSA and then the President asked about you this morning. Something about the investigation into Hakim Maheed's death? They all wanted to know if it was an official FBI investigation?" He took a long draw on his cigar and breathed in heavy smoke, letting the strong aroma from the

Dominican Republic tobacco leaves linger in his mouth, before releasing it, ever so slowly, as he exhaled.

Jimmy continued, "I told them all no, it was not an official investigation, because I know you would have briefed your Uncle Jimmy if there was anything he should know about. Is there something I should know about?"

They walked past a group of men smoking and making phone calls, since a signal could not be found inside the Kennedy Center tonight due to electronic blocking from the OPP. Nick watched Adriana approaching them, waving. She walked along the outside balcony with the slight evening breeze gently stirring her hair. Nick smiled at her and she at him.

"Yes, I do need to speak with you but tonight is probably not the place or the time. Can I call you tomorrow?"

"Yes, let's do that. Tomorrow, say lunch?" asked Jimmy.

"Sure," Nick answered as Adriana reached them. "Adriana, I would like to meet an old friend of the family, FBI Assistant Director, James Galloway."

"Nice to meet you, Mr. Galloway."

"Call me Jimmy, all my friends do. Are you having a good time this evening, Adriana?"

"Yes, sir I am. I have never been to an event—"

A dark young man, in a long flowing white Arabian robe, trimmed in gold, approached the group from the side. It was Prince Yasim with his entourage and his body guards. He abruptly interrupted Adriana, since she was only a woman and in his culture women did not matter much.

"Mr. Director. I just wanted to wish you congratulations. It is such an honor to be invited here this evening and here of all places, in the shadow of our Islamic Center and the Saudi Embassy. Have you ever seen our Embassy in all of its evening glory, Mr. Director?" The prince led them around the outside of the Center on the balcony while motioning for his associates and bodyguards to remain.

"Yes, many times but perhaps you would like to point it out for my young friends here. Prince Yasim, please allow me to introduce you to Mr. Nicholas Ryan an old friend and Special Agent with the FBI, and his date for this evening, Ms. Adriana Maheed. This is his Royal Highness, Crown Prince Yasim Ahmad of Saudi Arabia."

Nick shook his hand and the Prince stiffened slightly, before letting go and turning to Adriana. He leaned forward and kissed her hand. "*Salam*, good evening, Ms. Maheed," he said sweetly, before mumbling under his breath, *Sharmut*, meaning slut.

Nick heard the slur from the Prince and saw the light leave Adriana's eyes. He reached over and took her hand in his and squeezed it ever so softly. She breathed deep and smiled, squeezing his hand in return, saying, "Typical," under her breath.

"Good evening, your highness," said Jimmy.

"Ms. Maheed, please let me show you the glory of Saudi Arabia, you can see the building and our cultural center in all of its magnificence right from here." The group walked to the edge of the balcony and looked out over the city.

"Look," he continued, "There is the Saudi Embassy with over a thousand lights shining on our embassy, our crown jewel and over there is the Harry Truman building and directly across from here is the infamous Watergate building. Excuse me I must leave for a moment. I shall return."

Nick did not like the prince one bit, the arrogant ass. His cell phone rang, now free to accept any and all signals since they were outside of the protective bubble of the Center. He reached into his trouser pocket and pulled it out to answer, it was Tripp.

"Hey T.J., what's up?"

"Nick, I have been going through the list you gave me, you know the phone call list?"

"Yeah, what have you found out?" He walked away, leaving Jimmy leaning on the balcony enjoy his sinful cigar, alone. Adriana meandered behind Nick, enjoying the evening's fresh air and the wonderful sights and sounds of the capital. She was having the time of her life.

"Bad news I am afraid, my friend. Everybody that I have been able to track down on the list you gave me, is dead."

"Dead? What do you mean, dead?"

Adriana quickened her pace to catch up with him, when she heard the sound of alarm in Nick's voice. She wore a puzzled look on her face when she heard him say the words.

"Who?" she mouthed to Nick.

"Who's dead?" Nick asked Tripp.

"Well, just to name a few," Tripp continued to brief Nick in a somber tone, "Clarisse Dubois, Eduarte Manziales, Charles Ditten, Joseph Santino and a host of others. These are people from all over the globe. Dubois lived in Paris, Manziales was in Buenos Aries, Ditten is in Istanbul and Santino lived in Baltimore."

"You have got to be kidding. Are you sure of this?"

"Positive. There is one guy left. He lives in Baltimore but his roommate tells me he is away for the weekend. His name is Richard Palmer. Get to him quick, Nick. He is your only lead and the only one still breathing."

Nick faced Adriana's questioning face and he could see Jimmy behind her, alone, but still puffing on his old stogie.

"There is also something else that is really strange, Nicky. Your girlfriend's cell number does not appear anywhere on her father's call list. He never called her according to this list. Are you sure she is, who she says she is?"

Nick turned away from her. "I saw her picture on his desk, it was her."

"Could it have been altered? Not difficult to do nowadays with Photoshop. You know maybe figuring someone would come in to investigate and what better way than get close to the investigation than to impersonate the beneficiary and get inside information."

"Well, I did not ask for a driver license or an ID if that is what you are asking, T.J."

"Just play it safe. You don't know what you are dealing with here just yet, you know."

"I got you."

"Nick, another thing that is very strange. I checked one of the numbers with the phone company and they said it was a private VIP number and they would not release any info without a subpoena. Strange my friend, very strange."

"Who do you think the VIP is Tripp?"

"No idea but big, very important for the phone company to do that."

"Well, see what you can do…"

Nick saw Jimmy reaching into his tuxedo pants pocket to answer his cell phone.

Suddenly, all of Nick's internal alarm buzzers went off at the same time. He dropped his phone and ran to his old friend, not knowing why, just his gut instinct, nothing else, telling him something was wrong, dead wrong.

Nick screamed, "Jimmy, Jimmy, don't answer that pho—"

Jimmy looked at him in surprise; as he flipped open his cell phone. There was a brilliant flash of light and the deafening sound of an explosion, the power of which sent Nick Ryan reeling backward twenty feet.

Jimmy Galloway was dead in an instant, his upper torso blown away with the remains of his crumpled body crashing to the floor. Women's screams filled the night air.

• • •

The light in room #7707 at the Watergate Hotel went out and the door closed behind the departing guest. He was on his way back to his hotel room at The Grande, to get some much needed rest. It had been a long day. Then he would wait, wait for further instructions and the last name on his list to be added. He did not like staying in a city after he had made his hit but his employers were insistent, he had no choice if he wanted to get paid his bonus for making this very tricky hit.

• • •

Nick never heard the fire trucks, the ambulances, the police cars or anything else as they hustled him to the nearest hospital. They questioned him for hours in the recovery room but he could not really provide any information to help in their search for his old friend's murderer. The massive hunt was now on for the killer of James Galloway.

Chapter Twenty

John Nagle settled into the large leather seat onboard the Trans-Continental Airlines jet to London. He could finally rest and close his eyes. Although his victory was bittersweet, it had come in just the nick of time. His company was on the verge of a major breakthrough. His only regret was that his longtime wife Estelle was not there with him to share in his lifelong dream.

He had hit the big one. It was big by any standards and the gas flow projection meter finally stopped clicking when the estimates hit over sixteen trillion cubic feet of gas. And where there was gas you were sure to find oil. Now he was on a roll.

His next stop was to shore up the lease arrangements with WP Oil company to provide him with all of the drilling rigs they promised him. Without those rigs he was sunk. Fortunately, he was dealing with an honest, longtime oil man like himself, Sir Claude Hume.

He asked Hume once what he did to receive his knighthood and in typical dry English style he responded, "I pay my taxes. They seem to think if they knight you, you won't change your citizenship to a place where taxes are lower than sixty-percent." Funny, though, Nagle thought, they were right, he remained a British citizen.

"Champagne, sir?" said the pretty stewardess, interrupting his thoughts.

"Thank you. Miss, what time will we arrive in Heathrow?"

"We will be making our preparations for landing shortly, sir. Please buckle up."

The ride from Heathrow airport into London was one that Nagle always enjoyed. It went through the rolling countryside surrounding London, past the old and new factories until the journey brought him through the city center of London. The streets were always filled with people, day and night. He loved this city. The theater, the restaurants, the ballet, the financial district, the shops, but most of all the people.

He remembered the first time he'd taken his wife, Estelle, to London and they went to a Chinese restaurant in Chinatown and the small dining place only had chopsticks. Estie insisted on a knife and fork. By the time the owner was able to secure the proper utensils, she was an expert with the ancient apparatus. Nagle still chuckled anytime he thought of that evening.

What Nagle enjoyed most about his trips to London was staying at the Savoy. He liked the approach and anticipation of driving up to the hotel. The cab would turn off Charing Cross Road, then turn left onto the Strand and a few blocks later make the right to the Savoy.

At the end of the small side street stood a massive sign on a highly polished marquee over the hotel's entrance which simply said, *Savoy*. It was such a classy place with Bentleys and Rolls Royce cars parked along the entranceway, discreetly awaiting to take a guest to wherever they needed to go. It was such understated elegance which had always appealed to Nagle, especially now considering that he spent the last six months living in a field trailer. It was one of his rare indulgences.

"Good Morning, sir. Welcome to the Savoy. Are you checking in, sir?"

"Yes, I will be."

The greeter snapped his fingers crisply and a bellman rushed to relieve John Nagle of his burdensome luggage. He was now in the care of The Savoy.

"Welcome, sir. I hope you have an enjoyable stay. If you will follow the bellman he will lead you to the registration desk."

Nagle checked into the Savoy and asked if there were any messages left for him. The young Scotsman, whose nametag proclaimed he was Angus from Edinburgh, checked the special message box behind him at the front desk and checked for Nagle's room, room #1345 and retrieved a large stack of yellow message slips.

"These messages were in our arrival box waiting for you Mr. Nagle until you checked in."

"Thank you, Angus," he said and headed towards his room.

While riding the lift to his room, he sorted through all of the messages, some from Clark Wooden on site, six from his desperate ex-banker, William Newton, pleading with him to return his phone call. There were also messages of congratulations from other oilmen, and field workers asking for rig jobs but no messages from Sir Claude.

He had left a message for Claude before he departed the states, telling him he was coming to town and asking him for a sit-down meeting. He picked up the hotel phone and dialed seven, for room service.

"Yes, Mr. Nagle, welcome to the Savoy. This is Patrice, how may I help you?"

"Can you have them send three eggs over hard, some toast, jam not marmalade and some ham along with a glass of orange juice with a pot of coffee, black, no cream, no sugar. Okay? Do you have that?"

"Yes, sir. It will take approximately fifteen minutes to arrive in your room. Will there be anything else, sir?"

"No, thank you."

Nagle went into the bathroom and washed his face and pulled out his toothbrush and razor. He did not really feel alive until he completed both of those tasks in the morning, even though it was two in the afternoon, London time, it was still four a.m. Houston time.

He picked up the phone again and the operator was immediately at his beck and call. *I love this hotel*, he thought to himself. "Can you connect me to the office of Sir Claude Hume, Chairman of Westminster Petroleum at their Westminster headquarters?"

"Yes, sir, Mr. Nagle. Right away."

The phone rang only once, before a cheery voice answered, "Mr. Hume's office, Chelsea speaking. How may I help you?" Chelsea Borders was Sir Claude's longtime administrative assistant and his right arm. She grew up in the oil business with her father and older brothers who worked as roughnecks toiling on the grueling North Seas oil drilling platforms. She knew the business inside and out and started working with Sir Claude while he was managing the Norwegian drilling operations. He was a good boss.

"Hi Chels, this is Johnny."

"Johnny, is that you! John Nagle, it is so good to hear your voice. Where are you?"

"I'm at the Savoy."

"You mean you are here, in London?"

"Yes, I just got in an hour or so ago. I'm only staying for a day or so then I am off to the site in the Med."

"Oh my God. You should have called. I know that Claude would have loved to have seen you."

"I did call and left a message with Stephanie day before yesterday."

"Stephanie! That twit. She is planning her wedding to some barrister and that bloody wedding is all she thinks about. I will have to give her a real what for. But Johnny seriously, we had no idea you were coming."

"I really need to speak with Sir Claude, Chels. It's urgent."

"He is out of the country and out of touch. He has only called in once in the last fortnight. He's on one of those fancy hunt holidays in Russia. You know where they corral all of these animals on a couple hundred thousand acres and give everybody a rifle to shoot the poor defenseless things. Terrible."

"Can you get to him? Leave him a message? I really need to talk to him."

"Like I said, he is on some property in Russia, with some chap named Varinsky."

"Vladimir Varinsky?"

"Yeah, Johnny that's him. Sorry, dear. He won't be back for another week, but if he calls in I can tell him that you really need to speak with him."

"Thanks, Chelsea. I appreciate it."

"Okay, Johnny. But I tell you what, would you care to join me for dinner tonight, at my place, just like old times?"

"Sure," he said, remembering how caring and understanding Chelsea was when Estelle was sick and how they'd gotten to know one another better over the last six months.

"Seven? I'll pop on by and pick you up."

"I'll just have the hotel's car drop me off and save you a trip."

"Okay, Johnny."

"Great, looking forward to it, Chels. See you then."

John Nagle had gotten to know Chelsea Borders quite well over the last six months since his wife died. She would show him the town on his numerous visits to London to work with Sir Claude and his staff.

After many visits, they soon ran out of the usual tourist places to go and she began to make him dinner at her flat. A home cooked meal is something John Nagle cherished when traveling, because even at the best restaurants the food all started to taste the same after awhile.

The two of them would talk until the wee hours of the morning and the last time he had seen her, she kissed him on the cheek as he was leaving and one thing led to another. He stayed the night and when he left her apartment the next morning, she whispered, "Come back soon, Johnny. I miss not having you around."

Nagle arrived right on time, carrying a nice bottle of wine and looking forward to an enjoyable evening. They had a great meal and reminisced about the times gone by. Nagle left her apartment the next morning around four a.m. and headed back to his hotel room. Chelsea was still the sweetheart she had always been to him. He missed her already.

He would swing by London when he had to return to Houston. Yeah, that was a good idea. But he could not put her out of his mind. It was only then he realized, she was the real reason he came to London in person. He could have handled the details by phone but then he would not have seen Chelsea. Better late than never for him to realize his true feelings for her. He wasn't getting any younger.

Chapter Twenty-One

The hip boots rubbed against his thighs and the thick rubber made a high-pitched squeaking sound as he walked. Sir Claude was glad they were back on dry land.

"Whew, don't ever take me into that backwater again. That was terrible. The sound had to alert any animals for miles around that we were coming."

"Wait Claude, the best is yet to come," said Vladimir, nodding to his porter to bring forth the cold vodka.

These Russian think that vodka is the cure for everything, thought Claude. All he knew is that after a couple of nips of their heavy duty vodka and he was no good, no good for anything.

"Yes, Claude, try this. *Nostrovia!*"

"Cheers to you too, Vladimir."

"Now we get to the business, ya?"

"Ya."

They walked with their porters leading the way, breaking and cutting the tall brush and blazing the trial. They were on a hunt for wild boars and had only seen about ten of the small ones. If Vladimir considered a two-hundred pound, wild boar small, maybe Claude wished they wouldn't find any larger boars along this narrow trail.

"You company is takin' beatin in U.S., ya?"

"Ya."

"With that oil spill and all your profits are down and you have had to sell property, ya?"

"Ya."

"Well, we partners now in Sakhalin, here in Russia. It very big but think we get more oil if we drill more. It proven gas wells, ya?"

"Ya." *You kicked out Shell Oil and stole their oil fields after they sank billions into it. Some friend and partner you turned out to be.*

"Well, you have many idle drills, deep water drills sitting, costing you money, ya?"

"Ya. But those were promised by my company for the Nagle-Israeli Oil project. We can't back out now."

"Promised? They pay? They find gas? They find oil? We have oil, we need rigs, lots of rigs. How long you promise for?"

"They were held in reserve for them until this past Thursday."

"And now, promise over, ya?"

"Well, I know these people and I gave them my word that—"

"Claude, they no find gas, they no find oil. Ya? Let's make money, okay?"

The lead porter raised his hand and the others set the luggage down and fanned out into the tangled brush. Vladimir and Claude swung their shotguns from their shoulders and released the safety from their enormous weapons. The lead porter held up five fingers in the air, signifying he had a bead on a very large target ahead. On a scale of one to five, five was the biggest.

Hunting wild boars in the brush was very dangerous business. The boars would rush you lightning fast from the deep underbrush, and attack you with their razor sharp tusks, curved teeth capable of cutting a hunting hound in half. They were mean and they would just keep attacking, until you killed them or they killed you.

Claude could see nothing of what the porter was signaling about. But these porters were the best, having been imported from India where they had helped hunters track lions and rogue elephants on hunting expeditions.

The lead porter stopped, raised his fist in the air and pointed to his right. It was almost time. Claude could see nothing beyond the path in front of him. The brush on both sides was dense and impenetrable.

One could only hope there was just one boar because he had only one bullet in his Sterling boar gun. The weapon was beautiful in its design, with an engraved scrolled silver side bolt mechanism, oak stock and a kick that would throw a body to the ground if he were not used to it. The group of porters dispersed to the side and the lead one quickly raised his rifle, bringing down a two-hundred-fifty pound angry boar.

"So Claude, we have deal, you send us rigs, we all make money?"

As he was saying this, the largest boar they had seen on this trip was charging directly at Vladimir, who had his back to the wild beast.

"Claude, ya we have deal?"

The large bull boar was angry and the porters were nowhere to be seen. Claude raised his weapon but Vladimir was standing with his back to the charging boar, now between him and the charging monster boar.

"Move Vladimir, there's a huge boar and he is coming right at us. He's coming fast down the path," Claude yelled as the beast was charging them.

"We have deal Claude, ya?"

"Yes, we have deal, ya."

Vladimir spun around and planted a 308 Caliber bullet right between the eyes of the charging boar. The stunned wild animal, suddenly stopped and dropped dead right at the big Russian's feet.

"Now we celebrate with Root Vodka, the best stuff, ya?"

"Ya, now we celebrate, ya. But give me a *Boodles* and tonic, with some lime," replied a beaten down Sir Claude. "And lots of ice."

What was he going to tell his friend John Nagle? Then he felt better thinking that they would never find oil at the Israeli location. Nobody could find oil there, not even the great John Nagle. He felt somewhat better and decided just to drown his remorse in another shot of vodka. Besides, he had not heard about any strike there and Nagle was out of time. But try as he might, he just did not get comfortable with the whole situation.

Chapter Twenty-Two

Nick woke in a hospital bed two hours later with a splitting headache. He checked his body, looking for broken bones. He felt his hip, arms, legs, chest and neck—nothing broken. It was four a.m. He had to get out of there and go back to his hotel.

Adriana was sleeping in a chair in the corner of the room, still dressed in her evening gown, but minus the veil, looking lovelier than ever.

Movement caught his eye in the hallway outside his room. One of D.C.'s finest police officers was stationed at his door. Nick tried to move but groaned from the pain. The guard looked in and he took off, most likely to alert his supervisor that his Nick was awake.

The room was soon flooded by FBI Investigators, Bomb Squad Personnel, D.C. Metro Police, Secret Service, and a slew of others, all asking the same questions. What happened? Why was Nick running towards Director Galloway? Why was he not on the official guest roster? Why was he added late? What was his relationship with Jimmy Galloway? What was his relationship with Adriana Maheed? When one group was finished asking him questions another group would arrive and it started all over again.

Finally finished with the questions four hours later, Nick was discharged from the hospital. He and Adriana grabbed a taxi back to the Hyatt in Baltimore. She fell asleep in his arms in the back of the cab.

When they arrived at the hotel, Nick jumped into a hot shower. But even that didn't ease his mind. He still had a lot of questions going through his head. He dressed quickly then picked up his cell phone and called his father.

"Hi, Pop. It's me. You heard?"

"Yeah, one of the security guys came in and woke me this morning to tell me about Jimmy. How did you hear?"

"I was there, Pop, with Uncle Jimmy, right there in the heat zone, two seconds earlier and I could have saved his life. Damn, it's happening all over again. It was…terrible. One minute he was there and the next minute he was in a thousand pieces, splattered all over the glass walls. I don't know. I got to–! "He paused to calm himself for a minute.

"If you had gotten to him two seconds sooner, I would be coming to D.C. to attend two funerals. I don't know if I could handle that Nicky."

"Pop, you coming up for the funeral?"

"Yes. I'm not sure if they will let me fly yet but I'll be there, count on it. Jimmy was the best. He was good to both of us. Are you going to stick around for it?"

"Yeah, the funeral probably won't be for a couple for days so let me know what you want to do, okay Pop?"

"Yeah, Nicky. I'll talk to you later, son. Watch yourself. By the way I went by your apartment and a gal named Rosa left a message on your answering machine a couple of times looking for you. I left them on your machine. Is she the one with the DEA?"

His father stopped, waiting to get a response from his wayward son. When there was none he continued, "She sounds like nice girl. I think you may have this lady here stuck on you my boy. You better call her, you hear?"

"Yeah, I need to touch base with her. Thanks Pop. I have a lot of things going on, both here and there. I'll talk to you soon, okay Pop?

"Yeah son. Talk to you later."

Nick checked his cell and it showed that he had one missed text. He hit the pound button and a text message appeared on his phone, it was from Rosa. *Thinking of you. Be safe. Call me when you have a sec. Caring*— R.

Chapter Twenty-Three

Gandorf Gaskins, Gandy to most everybody in downtown Baltimore, was a long time Baltimore City cop, now a Homicide detective, with a foul temper and even fouler smell. He insisted on wearing the same grey suit for weeks on end, fully buttoned even during the scorching Baltimore summers. He sweated profusely and had permanent salt stains encircling the underarms of his suit jackets.

Gaskins was waiting in front of the hotel until he finally saw who he was looking for. Nick Ryan headed right toward him to retrieve his rental car.

"So there he is, the big hot shot FBI Special Agent, Nicholas Ryan."

"Hi, Gandy. How ya doing, Sergeant?" said the acquiescent Ryan, now in the clutches of the unwelcome and incompetent detective. He walked over to the old cop standing by the valet, who held open the door to Nick's rental.

"It's Detective Sergeant now, Agent Ryan. And don't you forget it."

Nick extended his hand to Gandy.

Gandy and Nick never got along since the day they met. When Nick was working on a murder-for-hire case in Baltimore and in Washington D.C. they had traced the connection directly to Gaskins. He denied knowing anything at all about the hits or being involved. Nick thought he was the trigger in a couple of the cases but could not prove it. But it did raise Gaskin's profile with the big brass in the department and Gandy's career never went anywhere after that incident.

"What the hell is that? I shake hands with friends and Nick you certainly are not my friend, at least not today."

Gaskins was tall, noted for his crooked teeth and crooked dealings. He had a partial head of grey hair, balding in the front and the back, racing to meet each other in the center of his head.

He walked with a slight limp, his detective limp he called it, for he had stopped a carjacking one evening. He was working uniform patrol at the time on The Block and was rewarded with a permanent bullet fragment in his left hip. As a result, the graying cop received a commendation from the Mayor ten years earlier and a promotion to Detective Sergeant - Grade One.

What they never revealed was, he was there to pick up a payoff from one of the bar owners. They just made sure he never made it beyond Detective Sergeant, Grade One. He took his dissatisfaction out on anyone he could bully, while most people would just avoid the tired old cop whenever they could.

"What do you mean?" asked Ryan, puzzled by the inquiry.

"You filed an insurance report with Global Insurance Company, saying Hakim Maheed's death was a homicide but you did not file a report with Baltimore City Police Department. I had to find out about it from the report filed by Global. You made me look bad, very bad, Agent Ryan. I would also like to talk to you about the death of Director Galloway."

"Detective Gaskins, you are way out of your jurisdiction and I spent hours talking to everyone and their brother about Galloway's death. He was also a very close friend and I don't know if I particularly like what you're inferring. Now if you'll excuse me, we have somewhere we have to be."

Ryan walked behind Gaskins and sat down in the car as Adriana slid into the seat next to him. "Got to go, Gandy. Good seeing you again." Ryan drove off and headed up I-83 heading towards the suburbs. The drive from downtown Baltimore to the suburbs wound through the old industrial parks and past old mansions, all built during Baltimore's glory days as a thriving maritime region.

The highway broadened out, adding four lanes, as it reached the fast growing suburbs, but Nick could still see the thriving developments built to house the growing government sector in downtown Baltimore.

Ryan was looking to talk to a computer geek named Ricky Palmer, who worked at a computer big box store in Cockeysville. He was the last one alive on Hakim's list. Palmer's roommate said they could find Palmer at work that day, but would be home later. Nick wanted to talk to him as soon as possible, and decided not to wait, since everything seemed to be moving faster and faster. He did not know how much time he had left.

"Nice fellow, your friend Gaskins," said Adriana sarcastically, laughing, as they pulled into the store's parking lot.

Nick had been quiet the whole drive up from the city and did not respond as they got out of the car.

"Is everything all right Nick?"

"No, it isn't."

"Talk to me."

"It's important we see Palmer first, then you and I need to talk."

"No, let's talk now." She stopped walking in the center of the parking lot and folded her arms, her mind made up she was going to get to the bottom of what was troubling Nick.

"Do you know a Clarisse DuBois?"

"Yes, she's my father's friend in Paris who I told you about. She was the girl in the photo on my father's desk."

"Was, his friend," said Nick.

"I don't follow. What do you mean she *was* his friend, Nick?"

"She's dead."

"Dead? Clarisse? Clarisse is dead? Why Nick? I don't understand?"

"Do you know an Eduarte Manziales?"

"Yes. My father and I were scheduled to visit him in Buenos Aires."

"He is also dead."

"Eduarte is dead? Nick what is going on? What's happening?"

"What about Frank Nitten? Ishwar Patek? Omar Rammer? Stanislaw Lebrun?"

"I don't know those names."

"Well, they are also dead. Plus others."

"What, why? I don't understand, Nick. Help me understand."

"All of these people had one thing in common, their names were on the list of people your father called from his cell phone, now they are dead. And I also forgot to mention that your father's neighbor, Joseph Santino was also on your father's call list."

"Oh my God!"

"Yes, these people had all been called by your father and are all now dead but what I don't understand is your name does not appear anywhere on your father's call list. He never called you?" Nick turned and started walking back towards the store. "I am going to need to have you explain that to me. We'll talk later. Ricky Palmer is the last person alive that was on your father's call list. We need to find him, while he's still alive."

The store was bustling with customers buying electronics for the upcoming Memorial Day holiday.

"Hi," said Nick to the sweet young twenty-something behind the customer service counter.

"Hi, back at you," she said, smiling. She looked like she could not have been more than seventeen.

"I'm looking for Ricky Palmer."

"Sure. Let me page him. He is working TVs today. You need anything else?" she said, returning to her flirty ways.

Give me a break, thought Nick. "No, just Ricky Palmer."

"I'll page him for you. RICKY PALMER, RICKY PALMER PLEASE COME TO THE CUSTOMER SERVICE COUNTER."

When he didn't appear she paged him again. "RICKY PALMER PLEASE COME TO THE CUSTOMER SERVICE COUNTER. CUSTOMER IS WAITING."

A few minutes later they saw him. He walked across the shiny white tile floor, with his shirt unbuttoned around his waist and his large belly poking out over his belt. He had a group of scraggly hairs on his chin surrounding his mouth, trying to resemble something of a goatee. His smudged name tag said *Ricky*.

"Yes sir, I'm Ricky. How can I help you?"

Ryan showed him a picture of Hakim Maheed and asked, "Have you ever seen this man before?"

"Sure. I did some private work for him off site. Neat stuff. How is the old dude?"

"He's dead."

"What?"

"You heard me, he's dead. And anyone who has been in touch with him has also been showing up dead and I might add your name is on that list." Nick could see that Ricky Palmer was visibly shaken, finding out that his former client, Hakim Maheed, was dead but also that he could be next. His knees began to shake.

"Calm down, Ricky. You are safe, for the moment. Just help me out here, will you?"

"Sure, sure, I'll tell you anything you want to know. He's dead? Really?"

"Yeah, Ricky. Now focus, it is very important. What kind of work did you do for him?"

"He brought in an encrypted flash drive with some videos on it and wanted it real bad. The dude paid two-hundred bucks for me to crack the encryption. Cracking the encryption was a piece of cake but then I found it had a different operating system, some Far Eastern crap, if you know what I mean, so I had to convert it to the good old U.S. of A. gold standard."

"What did you do with it?"

"Well he came in the next day and asked me to copy it on to one of our flash drives and then left. So I copied it onto one of our Digi-Tex flash drives and gave both of them to him."

"Did you see what was on it?

"It was video."

"Did you make a copy?"

"No copies, that's unethical, besides who cares? But I did watch a minute or so of it, just to make sure the conversion worked okay."

"What was it?"

"Dumb stuff."

"Yeah, like what Ricky?"

"It was a meeting of some sort, very dark, looked like it was in a cave or tent or something. A big tall dude, a camel jockey, standing in front of a bunch of young guys all dressed in robes but like he was speaking English. Weird. The old dude, Maheed, he kept muttering the word, *Kitman*, out loud, absentmindedly, like he thought it may mean something to me."

Adriana tensed at the sound of the word and asked the young techie, "What did he say?"

"He muttered the word *Kitman* or *Kidman* or something like that. You know like Nicole Kidman, the movie star," Ricky said.

"What else did he say? What did you see in the video?"

"Well, in the video, all these guys were all sitting around in front of this Arab looking guy, with a long white robe, beard and all, you know like he was their teacher and…"

Ricky was interrupted by the store's loudspeaker announcing, "RICKY PALMER, RICKY PALMER, PLEASE COME TO THE CUSTOMER SERVICE COUNTER. YOU HAVE A CUSTOMER PHONE CALL. RICKY PALMER, PLEASE COME TO THE CUSTOMER SERVICE COUNTER. CUSTOMER WAITING."

"I'll be right back. I got to take that call."

They watched him walk away, and disappear behind the customer service area. "What do you think?" asked Adriana.

"I would love to get my hands on whatever it was. What I don't know is if that was in the shoe box we have been searching for. We'll ask him about it when he comes back."

Several minutes later an announcement came over the loudspeaker, "CODE 9, CODE 9 TO CUSTOMER SERVICE, STAT!! CODE 9, CODE 9 TO CUSTOMER SERVICE, STAT!!"

Nick saw six to eight, white shirted employees make a mad rush towards the customer service counter and he got an uneasy feeling in his stomach. Once again he did not like coincidences and this gave him a bad feeling, a very bad feeling.

"I don't like this, not one bit," he told Adriana. "Let's check it out."

A crowd had formed around the hallway near the rear of the store and they could not see what was going on. They pushed their way through and as they got to the front of the line they heard the police sirens and saw the red lights twirling at the front of the store.

This is not good at all, thought Nick.

He heard a distraught woman wailing, telling those around her, "One minute he was helping me next thing I know he is laying on the floor."

Nick looked over the shoulder of the guy standing in front of him and could see the big geek dead, lying in a pool of blood on the floor. *Damn.* All he did was do what he did best and he paid for it with his life.

"I want to check the security camera, Wait here," Nick told Adriana.

"Yeah, that's a good idea."

He made his way to the second floor security area and a big beefy cop was standing guard. Nick flashed his FBI credentials and was allowed to pass with a grunt and disgusted look by the big cop.

The cops inside the overcrowded security room, crammed with video monitors covering the store, were all hunched over a video monitor watching Ricky walk down a hallway. Soon they could see a hand raised behind his head, holding a gun with a silencer. They saw Ricky fall to the floor, dead. The assassin was never seen in the video.

He's a pro, thought Nick. He knew exactly what he was doing and exactly where the cameras were panning. *Time to leave.*

He met Adriana in the hallway. "It was a hit," he whispered.

"I think it is best if we get out of here. This place will be swarming with more cops in a minute and to be connected to two murders within twenty-four hours will certainly raise some eyebrows. Come on, I know a place nearby where we can get a cup of coffee and figure out what we are going to do next."

If only they had another five minutes with Palmer, he'd probably still be alive.

They left the rear of the store past the police laying a large sheet over Ricky, the dead young techie. Three more cops cordoned off the parking lot, to begin their investigation.

Adriana looked away from the scene on the sidewalk and told him, "Please let's go."

Nick drove the ten blocks down York Road, turned down Aylesbury and pulled into the Bay Coffee Company's parking lot. He ordered two lattes, while Adriana grabbed a table near the rear of the small store. It was a refuge as a quiet place to go, to talk or read at the small wooden tables. They never rushed their customers.

Nick set the aromatic, steaming latte coffee in front of Adriana, sat down and looked at her, saying, "If only we had some more time with Ricky. He was the only person other than your father who has seen that video. What's on it that would cause people to die?"

"What do you think is on the video, Nick?"

"Maybe it is not a what, but a who? Who is on the video that someone is looking to protect and will go to such great lengths to protect? They want the video bad, real bad. I don't know, but the number of people who are dying continues to multiply. And what is the connection with the video, Ricky Palmer and the death of Jimmy Galloway? Their only connection, that I can see, is your father's phone calls from his cell phone."

She looked up at him, her eyes betraying her fear, "Everybody my father calls seems to be turning up dead, Nick. That is scaring me."

Nick sipped his coffee and looked up at her.

"Adriana when I spoke to my friend Tripp he was checking out all of the calls your father made from his cell phone. Can you tell me why your name or your number does not appear on your father's log anywhere? There is no record of him calling you. Why is that?"

Adriana looked seriously at Nick, "My father had been working away from his home because he told me he wanted to work on it in secret. He always called me from the cabin." She looked down on the old wooden table, stirring her coffee, while talking about her father.

"Cabin? What cabin?" asked Nick incredulously.

"The cabin in the picture, you know, the one where we were standing by the Lake. Deep Creek Lake, it's out in Western Maryland."

"But it never showed up in any land records your father owned."

"Oh. It was listed in my name. My father gave me the place as a gift, a place to get away from it all but he used it more than anyone."

Nick believed her, he needed to believe her.

"Drink up, we're leavin'."

"Where are we going?"

"We're going to your father's cabin at Deep Creek Lake, that's where. Everything keeps pointing back to that box. We need to find the box, that's the key. The longer we wait the more danger we will be in." They pulled away from the parking lot and headed towards I-70 West, for the nearly four hour drive to Deep Creek Lake.

"Who is Kitman?" asked Nick after they'd been driving for a while on the deserted highway, heading towards the Western Maryland mountains.

"It is not a who but a what."

"Okay, then what is a Kitman?"

Adriana turned away, watching the rolling hills and lush green fields of suburban Maryland go rushing by, a beautiful and calming sight to behold. The horse country passed them by with its beautiful white board fences stretching as far as the eye could see. The young colts could be seen running along the fences in a mock race to the mythical finish line.

Finally, turning back to Nick, she told him, "In our beliefs, it does not matter what you say with your words, it only matters what is in your heart."

"Are you saying they condone outright lying?"

"Yes, but it goes much deeper than that. You can lie to those outside of the faith. There are two forms of lying to non-believers that are permitted under certain circumstances, *Taqiyya* and *Kitman*. They are both used to advance the cause—in some cases by gaining the trust of non-believers in order to draw out their vulnerability and defeat them."

"What is the difference?"

"*Kitman* is lying by omission, or leaving out key information and *Taqiyya is* saying something that isn't true. The early deceivers were sent as scouts to spread the word about the approaching armies of our faith, to lull their enemies into a false sense of security are called *Kitmans*."

Nick had never heard the term before. "So, what are you saying?"

Adriana looked at him cautiously before continuing, "*Kitmans*, are allowed to lie to unbelievers in order to defeat them. Leaders in our world routinely say one thing to English-speaking audiences and then something entirely different to their own people in Arabic. Yassir Arafat, when he was alive, was famous for telling Western newspapers about his desire for peace with Israel, then turning right around and whipping Palestinians into a hateful and violent frenzy against Jews." She stopped talking as Nick made the turnoff from I-70 onto I-68, the final leg of their journey.

She continued to explain the depths of the conspiracy, "Another example of lying is using deception to trick your enemies into letting down their guard and exposing themselves to slaughter by pretending to seek peace or pretending to be one of them. The 9/11 hijackers practiced deception by going into bars and drinking alcohol, thus throwing off potential suspicion that they were fundamentalists plotting *jihad*. This effort worked so well, in fact, that even weeks after 9/11, John Walsh, the host of a popular American television show, said that their bar trips were evidence of hypocrisy but it was really *Kitman* at its finest."

"Really?"

"Yes. On one of the planes it was reported that the transmission from Flight #93 records the hijackers telling their doomed passengers that there is "a bomb on board" but that everyone will "be safe" as long as "their demands are met."

Obviously none of these things were true, but these men, who were so intensely devoted to the cause that they were willing to *slay and be slain for the cause of their beliefs*, saw nothing wrong with employing *Taqiyya* in order to facilitate their mission of mass murder. That is their belief."

"What does that have to do with your father and with the box we are searching for?"

"I don't know. I can't really piece it all together. *Kitman*, the cave, the men in robes, the students it all doesn't make sense. Maybe we will find some answers at the cabin," she said as Nick turned off highway I-68 and drove south onto a four lane highway, the gateway to the Western Maryland lake community.

They stopped at a small country roadside grocery store just off the main road and picked up some food, wine and provisions for their short stay. The manager turned out the lights behind them and went home to his waiting supper.

Nick drove past the nearly empty Garrett County Airport and after another fifteen minutes of stopping and slow driving, Adriana shouted, "Nick, here, turn here!" Nick nearly passed the entrance, driving by it in the dark.

He turned and inched his way onto a deserted dark road and navigated the small dirt path, with twists and turns before it stopped at a dead end at the lake and a small cabin off in the distance. There were no streetlights, no houses, no sign of life anywhere until they came upon the lone cabin at the very end of the road.

"We're home," said Adriana exultantly. The temperature had dropped over ten degrees in the high mountains and Adriana shuddered as she left the car.

"It's cold here in the mountains. I am surprised that I remembered how to get here, its been so long. "

"This place does have heat doesn't it? And electric?" Nick asked skeptically.

"All of the comforts of home. It has gas propane heat and even running water and a bed," flashed Adriana, searching for the cabin key.

• • •

An old blue Ford F-150 pickup slowed behind them on the main road at the top of the hill, and stopped briefly before driving away. The truck parked on a side road not far from the cabin. The driver turned off the ignition, lit a cigar and sat, waiting. His partner sat in silence, watching.

Chapter Twenty-Four

"It's just as I remembered it," said Adriana opening the door to the cabin, after retrieving the key from under the Mexican flower pot on the old wooden porch.

"How original of a hiding place," Nick told her.

"We actually left it unlocked for over a year once and nobody bothered it. My father has been using this place as his retreat to do his research and he'd been spending a lot of time here." The cabin was dark and had a smoky fireplace smell which permeated the still night air of the deserted cabin.

"Let me get the lights. It's propane gas and it's a little tricky," said Adriana.

When the gas lights flickered on, they revealed a large open room, with a fireplace off to the left side. An old bearskin rug lay spread out in front of it, facing an age old green sofa with dark small brown pillows stuffed in the corner.

The kitchen was small by any standard, with a small dining table and two wooden chairs at the very rear of the cabin. The dining table overlooked the rear window, showing the moon glistening off the lake beyond. A motorboat was tied to the dock and lay there listlessly bumping the sides against the dock.

"That is the community boat for all the homes here on the cove. They keep it here and everybody pays to keep it maintained. There are not a lot of homes here on the cove, so we have plenty of privacy. But this time of year there is nobody around, it's deserted," Adriana explained.

She pointed to the two doors to the side. "That door is to the bedroom and the other one, here to the left, is the bathroom."

"I think we should both search the place top to bottom and see if what we are looking for is here," Nick said scanning the room.

"What are we looking for?"

"It could be a flash drive, a chip, a notebook, a shoe box, anything we find that does not belong here. Tripp told me it's about the size of a shoe box, with a biohazard emblem and some Arabic writing on the top. Other than that I am at a loss. This is the last place to look and from the looks of it we can search this place rather quickly."

"Let's start with my father's desk, if it is anywhere it would be there."

"Good idea," said Nick as he scoured the tiny cabin starting with Hakim's desk. On the desk there was a notepad with some numbers on it, a calendar with initials scribbled on the border but nothing else of any value. Nick knelt down and looked under the bottom of the drawer and saw a small key taped to the underside. He peeled it off.

"Any idea what this opens?" Nick held up the key for Adriana to see.

"No, I've never seen it before, sorry Nick."

Nick checked the bedroom, the bathroom, the walls and the floors for any hidden panels, nothing. The bedroom had a large bed inside, much too large for the room but Nick was unable to find any hidden panels underneath or in the walls. Nick went back and searched the cabin again and again for a third time and still found nothing other than the small key with no home. Adriana had the same luck.

Nick was totally dejected, he did not like to lose and not finding this box was losing.

"Why don't you start a fire in the fireplace to take the chill off the room and I'll start making us something to eat?" Adriana said.

"Sure. Where's the firewood?"

"There is a small trap door to the left of the fireplace and you can just grab the logs through the trap door from inside. It keeps the wood dry and makes it easier to start a fire during the winter and you don't have to go outside in the snow."

"Sounds good to me," said Nick pulling on the small trap door handle.

"I don't know where else the box could be Nick," said Adriana from the kitchen, as the roaring fire began to warm the small cabin.

Nick stared at the small trap door, frowning. He tapped the walls searching for any hidden compartments. No luck.

"Dinner's ready," said Adriana, coming out of the kitchen with her father's laptop. She turned on her father's computer, but found that it was totally blank.

"Nothing," said a disappointed Nick, surveying the small cabin while opening an Australian Viognier, the perfect companion to her pasta and canned clams dish.

He poured two glasses of wine and they ate in silence, now at the end of their quest. "I really thought it would be here," a dejected Nick finally said. "I don't know where else to look, Adriana. We have to find it. I really thought it would be here. I was certain of it. It's the key to the whole thing. The key to why everything is happening." He slowly turned the key over and over in his hand.

"Nick, you went above and beyond, I could not ask for anything more. You cleared my father's good name by proving he did not commit suicide. I can't thank you enough for doing that for him."

Nick threw more logs onto the fire and again soon had a roaring inferno, warming the entire cabin. He loved making a fire in a fireplace, it reminded him of home, growing up. His father would save the largest piece of firewood for Thanksgiving dinner and would throw it on when they sat down to eat. It would burn and flame for hours.

He and Adriana settled in, sitting on the soft, warm bearskin, in front of the fire.

"Did your father shoot this bear?" Nick asked.

"Yes, in Iran a number of years ago. Then he had it shipped here. He was very proud of it."

Nick felt the rumpled, coarse hair between his fingers, as Adriana gently moved the lock of hair that had drifted to his forehead, brushing it back by his ear. When she finished, she stopped, not saying a word, she looked at him with her dark, dangerous eyes.

Adriana was close, so very close. He could smell the sweet scent of her perfume and peered into the depths of her eyes. She kicked off her shoes, to make herself comfortable, causing her skirt to hike high on her thighs, exposing her long athletic legs. She snuggled next to him, her hand twisting the blond hairs on his chest while they talked and talked, but none of their words made sense to either of them.

Nick leaned over and kissed her, softly, gently and sweetly. His hand slid around her neck and he continued to kiss her. He missed the touching, oh how he had missed it, as it all came rushing back. A tide of emotions swept over him, they were all good feelings.

She moved closer and kissed him with passion, pressing closer and closer, deeper and deeper.

He met her passion with passion. His feelings for her rose. He could feel the total warmth of her body, her breathing was faster and deeper.

Suddenly she stood, towering over him, she held out her hand and said knowingly, "Come. Come with me."

The lights in the cabin went out, but the two pair of eyes in the nearby pickup truck continued their vigil. *Time was running out. It would all be over soon.* The two men would wait and they would have their chance. The cigar smoke slowly drifted out of the truck window, rising high above it in the cool evening air. Soon.

Chapter Twenty-Five

Nick awoke while it was still dark outside, to the smell of brewing coffee coming from the kitchen and the sound of singing in a language that was unfamiliar to him. *"Gharibe ashena dustet daram bia…poshte divare delam ye sedaye pa miad…"* It was more like humming than singing he thought. He dressed and soon found Adriana in the kitchen frying eggs, wearing his dress shirt, and a pair of pink fluffy bedroom slippers adorned her feet.

"Pretty song from a pretty lady. What were you singing?"

"It was a peasant song my mother taught me as a child. It is the story of a young man visiting a village to find a wife. He has to choose between two sisters, one is beautiful and one is very smart. He chooses the smart one, for he knows that beauty is only skin deep but with intellect all things are possible."

"Very nice. I liked it."

"I'm glad. I could always tell when my parents made love. My mother would sing this song the next morning. I see why she sang it now. Coffee?"

"I'd love some coffee. I'll restart the fire and throw some logs on the fireplace to warm us up." Nick opened the side trap door and restarted the fire while picking up the used wine glasses from the floor. He glanced at where they had sat on the bearskin rug last night, his mind now full of wonderful memories.

"We can stay here for awhile if you like, Nick, if you have nowhere to rush to. What do you say? We can go into town get some clothes, buy some more food, some more wine, fish in the lake and have a very nice time."

"I have never had a better invitation," he said and walked towards her. A floor board squeaked under his full weight. He froze. Quickly pulling up the bearskin rug and pushing it aside he felt the floor for any telltale sign of a secret compartment. He pushed on the longest board, than another, then another and finally the one next to it popped up. Adriana was soon by his side, still holding her spatula, looking over his shoulder.

"What is it, Nick?"

"I'm not sure, but we will soon see."

He shifted the wide board out of the way and at the bottom of the cavity underneath, was a grey metal box the size of a shoebox. There was a biohazard symbol emblazoned on the top on one side and Arabic writing on the other.

"Can you read that, Adriana? What does it say?"

"Yes," she said, falling silent. "It says, *Kitman.*"

Nick looked at her and slowly lifted the box from its hiding place, hoping it was not booby trapped. He set it on the desktop, finally looking at what he had been searching for since he'd come to Baltimore.

"What do we do?" asked Adriana.

"The smart thing to do is to take it to the nearest Army Biohazard facility, like Aberdeen Proving Grounds and let them handle it."

"Is that what we are going to do?"

"No," said Nick reaching into his pocket, retrieving the small key that he had found the day before, hidden underneath Hakim's desk drawer. "I said that is the smart thing to do, I did not say that's what we are going to do."

Nick inserted the key and tried to turn it. It did not work.

"Can I try?" asked Adriana. She pushed the key in again just a little further and turned. They heard a click and the lock opened. He stepped to the front of the metal shoebox and slowly lifted the lid. Inside the small grey box were papers and photos and documents, pictures and receipts. Nick was glad that the biohazard emblem was a phony meant to scare off the curious and did not appear to pose any harm to them.

At the bottom of the box he retrieved a small plastic bag and found what he was looking for—what Ricky Palmer had died for yesterday. Inside the bag was a flash drive with the brand name, Digi-Tex on the side.

"Bingo," exclaimed Nick. "Let's put this into your father's computer."

The computer was agonizingly slow to start up and to read the chip. The video began. It was an amateur video taken in what appeared to be either a tent or a cave. Drapes or dark sheets were hung everywhere to disguise its location. They could hear chants in the background.

The lighting quality of the video was poor at the beginning but soon improved as more and more lights were turned on. A muffled Arabic voice, obviously a man's voice came over the small screen making pronouncements, something that Adriana instantly translated.

"This is a meeting with our Saviors and the Mentor." The tall man in the front of the class sat down crossed legged before his group of some twenty students. Nick froze at the sight of the man on the screen; it was the devil himself– Osama Krazir. Nick was amazed that Ricky Palmer did not recognize the most hated man in the United States.

"What is he saying to them?" Nick asked the equally shocked Adriana.

"It is very tough to hear, let me turn up the volume. There that's better. He is welcoming them…

"*Welcome my students. Today you finish what you came here for, but your journey and work has just begun. While I know that most of you here feel that you would prefer to join the suicide warriors across our world, your calling is much higher. Those brave warriors, who willingly gave their life to our cause, are but like mosquitoes to a camel. They can annoy and distract the camel but they cannot kill the camel.*"

"*We must use our superior intellect to defeat and kill this beast. Because our cause is just, we will not be defeated. We must pluck this Israeli thorn from our side and be rid of them once and for all. But first the camel must be brought to their knees. The way to kill the Yankee camel, the protector of the Israelis is the same way you kill the desert camel, give them what they want. Make them pay."*

"If you give a camel too many apples every day he cannot digest it. His stomach will turn on him and be his own worst enemy and the camel will die."

The group of students applauded Krazir as he continued. His voice rose to a fever pitch and while Nick did not understand the words he was saying, he had seen early videos of Hitler addressing crowds and had the same feeling from those videos that he was having now. He was a masterful speaker, just not a speaker for the right cause, thought Nick.

Nick looked at Adriana and she said, "He sure knows how to whip up a crowd, doesn't he?"

"Yes, he does."

The computer screen flickered, nearly going dead. It was being run on battery power, since Adriana could find no power cable at the cabin. Soon, the screen flickered back on and the video resumed.

Calming the students, Krazir continued, *"Many of you here have special assignments, these duties are of great import to our cause. You will go among them, be in the lion's den, be with them, be like them, and be one of them. You will need to embrace them to defeat them.*

Remember, that if they ask of you your beliefs, you are a Kitman and you must deny all. It only matters what is in your soul, not what is on your lips. Remember that and you will succeed. Make the Americans pay, bring them to their knees. Bankrupt them. It will not be hard or take much time. You must persevere, you must have patience, then soon they will not have the energy or resources to support Israel. Then we will be victorious and we will pluck the festering thorn from our side."

The students went wild cheering. He stood and quieted them. The pep talk was over, and one by one the students rose to pay homage to their mentor.

The computer flickered, died and after many false starts it finally churned to a stop and could not be restarted again.

"We need to see the end of this video. We need to see why so many people had to die," said Nick.

"You see if you can find a power cable for this in my father's desk. I have my laptop in the car," said Adriana. "I'll go get it." She grabbed Nick's red jacket to keep her warm in the dark cool mountain air. She pulled the hood up over her head, and made her way to the front door.

Nick could feel the rush of the cold air come through the cabin door, as she pulled it open. She turned to him to say with a grin, "Don't go away, big boy. I'll be right back."

Nick smiled at her while she turned to head outside. But she didn't make it past the threshold. She was cut down by a barrage of bullets which hammered into her body.

The first high powered bullet hit her high in the shoulder spinning her around. The second one, zeroing in as she turned, falling to the ground, hit her in her skull, shattering the left side of her face. The third sniper bullet was right on target, blasting a hole through her heart. Adriana was dead before she hit the ground inside the cabin.

Nick could see her there on the floor, a pool of blood running towards him from her head, soaking the once trophy bearskin rugs with her precious life source. He rushed to her, grabbing the nearby towel, trying to stop the bleeding. The barrage of bullets were ripping out over his head and puncturing the wooden floor and wall next to him, while he crouched down next to her. He kicked the door shut with his foot.

He looked at her face, her once beautiful face as he cradled her head in his hands. He could see what was left of her face, the lights in her life now gone, the twinkle in the eyes he had grown to cherish, forever silenced. He gasped at the sight of her now lifeless body laying there before him.

"Adriana, Adriana," he moaned

Bullets flew through the air, no longer the precision munitions that had butchered Adriana but now the lethal bombardment of automatic weapons flooded the cabin, ripping everything to shreds. The gunfire was incessant, raking the walls, the ceiling, the floor, and the desk. Nick moved Adriana to the side wall, unable to let go of her now lifeless body. He took one last look at her and he kissed her forehead before saying his goodbyes.

Staying low, he ran to the rear of the cabin looking for an escape route. The closed door offered only a temporary reprieve and the sense of safety was soon gone as the door was ripped apart and riddled with gunfire, tearing the old wooden door to shreds.

Nick had to get out of there but first he needed the chip. He crawled over the floor and pressed the chip release, it did not eject. Bullets continued to ricochet off the walls, shattering everything.

He tried again, this time the bullets were coming closer and also from the rear of the cabin. Nick tried a third time and finally the small chip popped out and into his hand. He could hear the assassins yelling in the front of the cabin and voices were closing in from the rear. He was trapped.

Nick saw the firewood trap door on the side of the small cabin and crawled towards it on his belly, taking one last look at Adriana lying in her pool of blood. He stopped for a minute thinking irrationally about bringing her, somehow. He could not just leave her here. The fusillade of bullets continued to rip overhead.

An incoming round shot out the gas light in the kitchen and he could see her no more. He hurried over by the fireplace, next to the trap door leading outside, he just barely fit through the opening for the firewood and he made his way outside. Fresh air.

It was still dark outside but his eyes soon adjusted to the darkness. The sound of gunfire filled the forest around him but he knew it would offer him no help, out here in the middle of nowhere. There was no one around. He had to get away.

Bullets continued to rack the cabin with automatic weapon fire, as he made his way to the lake. *If only he could get to the lake and to the boat.* It was up ahead, he could see it in the moonlight. He ran hard and then stumbled in the dark, tripping over some trashcans, making a racket as he headed towards the lake.

When he reached the boat dock Nick heard a loud explosion coming from the direction of the cabin. He turned to see a fireball rising above the spot where Adriana's family cabin had once been and where he had shared special moments with her. His thoughts were shattered by the sound of bullets ricocheting off the old wooden boat dock. They must have heard the trashcans and now they'd found him.

He untied the tender ropes and made for the ignition. The old Chris Craft started right up and soon he was pulling away for the shore, fast. They saw him. The bullets cracked the waters all around him, splitting the nearby waves in half. Nick turned and saw two men standing on the boat dock, before they ran back towards the burning cabin.

Nick steered the boat toward the city lights on the other side of the wide lake. He could see headlights on the lake road behind him coming from the cabin he had just left, coming around fast, trying to intercept him. He pushed the lake boat to full throttle and the eager Chris Craft racer surged ahead.

Suddenly, Nick saw the welcome sign of red and blue, police lights stopping the vehicle that was chasing him, before it made it to the bridge. He had a reprieve. But he was at a disadvantage, they knew what he looked like but he didn't know anything about them.

After tying up the boat on the pier on the other side of the lake, he was grateful he had made it to the other side of the lake. He looked back at the cabin still burning brightly in the forest. She was gone before he ever got the opportunity to really get to know her. He would not wait the next time, he would let his feelings be known, or should he just swear off loving anyone, play it safe, he asked himself. Time would tell him, he thought. Time to get a move on and fast.

For now, Nick had to see the rest of the video. There was something on it that people did not want anyone to know about. What was so important to cause the death of all these people? Whoever was searching for him would look for him at the hotel. He had to find out what the chip contained and headed to the only safe place left to him, home.

Chapter Twenty-Six

Sir Claude Hume sat silently in the rear of his car as it drove in a steady stream of rain towards Westminster Petroleum's World Headquarters in Westminster, a chic suburb of London. He'd spent a long fortnight with his wily Russian comrade.

Everyone at the home office would surely congratulate him when they heard the news about the agreement he had signed with the Russians. Then, why didn't he feel good about it? What troubled him the most was the headlines of the front page of the London Times, *Israel Discovers Mammoth Oil Find! Nagle Oil is prime beneficiary.*

He was sure that he would have a number of phone messages waiting for him when he reached his office, including ones from his old friend, John Nagle. The big limousine pulled into the parking garage in the basement of the building and Sir Claude took the Executive Elevator to the top floor.

Damn him, he cursed. How could he let the Russians put him in this position? He would have to call John Nagle and tell him he could not have the rigs. That was one phone call he did not wish to make. John and him went way back. There had to be some way out of this. There had to be some way for him to help Nagle and the Israelis. The answer would come in due time no doubt, he thought.

The elevator door opened and his longtime assistant, Chelsea Borders greeted him at his office door, with his tea and newspaper in hand. "Did you see the paper today? Did you see the headlines? Johnny found the big one. That is why he was here last week."

"John Nagle was here, here in London?"

"Yes, sir. He came in just to see you last week."

Claude dropped his head; this was going to be worse than he originally thought. *Did Varinsky know about this huge gas discovery? Did the Saudis? Is that why the Russians pushed so hard for the rigs?* He stood in his office overlooking the city of London below him.

It was so calm here, so orderly, he missed the old days when Wildcatters like him and John Nagle found oil by the seat of their pants and made fortunes for himself and everyone else. Now everything was done by engineers, computer simulations and the like. He could give a damn about this. Maybe he should just join John Nagle on his discovery journey? It would be real short lived if Nagle could not get his drilling rigs.

Claude pondered, *What can I do?* He looked over the Westminster Petroleum global drilling map, so prominently displayed in his office. It listed the location of every single rig, discovery well, closed field, and exploration areas around the world.

On the map he saw a big red circle around the area off the Louisiana coast. It was an area which had once been WP's pride and joy and a major activity area. Now, after the blowout of the Deep Water Sunset drilling rig it would be years before those wells could be reopened and would be operational.

That explosion was a black mark on his soul and on his record. Nobody remembers when he fought with the board to do their annual maintenance on the rig but no, no, they did not want to lose two weeks' worth of production out of their most prolific well. Now everybody was running for cover and pointing the finger of blame right at Sir Claude Hume. Well, the buck stops here, so to speak. He should have fought them harder. Safety always came first, except to his board. Now the damn American banks owned everything they had in the States and it had gotten real sticky. A real sticky wicket. Even if he could find extra drills, who would pay for them and why would anyone ever consider doing such a thing?

He saw the suddenly shapely Chelsea, waltz past his office door and he could swear he heard her humming a lyrical tune. She even looked different then he remembered. Then he remembered John Nagle had been in town a few days before and she had always been sweet on Nagle. Yes, how could he have been so dumb. Now he knew exactly what he was going to do! It was all starting to fall into place. He had found his answer for all his problems.

"Chelsea, can you get me Lee Chin in Hong Kong, then get me John Nagle on the phone? And Chelsea, pack your bags and all of your pretty dresses, you are going to Israel!"

Chapter Twenty-Seven

Moscow was very cold, even in May, as Vladimir Varinsky's chauffeured limo pulled in front of the large building which housed his office: The Office of the Soviet Oil Ministry. The limo passed a uniformed guard, who saluted as the car drove past. The black Russian limousine rode rough over the cobblestone driveway and turned around inside the large circular courtyard with a fountain in the center still off since last fall. The limo stopped in front of the large double glass doors in the building, while the old doorman hobbled over to open one of the double glass doors.

Karlov, his chauffeur of the last three years, parked and leaped to open the door for his most important passenger. Vladimir had lost his last chauffeur when his Mercedes Limo was attacked by Chechen separatists with a car bomb, intent on killing him.

How dumb they were, they did not even bother to check to see if he was in the limo at the time. He was still with one of his many mistresses but the bomb destroyed the car and killed his longtime driver. The Internal Security Apparatus (ISA) took care of the rebels and they were never heard from again.

After that incident, Vladimir, replaced his Mercedes limo with the old trusty standby, the Russian Zil. It was a huge car, weighing over five tons because of all the armor built into it. The massive car was built in very limited numbers but he liked the roomy rear area where he could entertain his lady friends and he much preferred the cloth seats and the privacy of the heavy drapes which adorned the rear compartment. The limo cost well over $300,000, U.S., more than the cost of forty Ladas, the car preferred by the everyday Russian and the only one they could afford.

It had been good to get away from Moscow, even if it was only for a few weeks. He could have anything he wanted because of his position in the Oil Ministry, which was gushing with Russian petrodollars.

He could have anything except the one thing he really sought, which was to leave Russia permanently. *Soon,* he told himself, looking through the notes, phone messages and newspapers left on his desk by Slvetna, his long time assistant. He always thought she worked for the KGB or their new replacement agency, The Directorate, different name, same people, same crude methods.

But now, he smiled to himself, more pleasant matters indeed. Vladimir always got what he wanted, as he pulled out the agreement which Sir Claude had signed.

He poured himself a shot of vodka to celebrate. Not only would he make money on the drilling, but he stood to profit on every drop of oil pumped in the Western fields. He received his kickback which was deposited in the Nationale Swiss Bank located in the Grand Caymans. This deal was even sweeter, since the Saudis paid him very, very well to steer the drilling capacity and equipment suppliers away from the Israelis. They did not want the Israelis to drill at all, anywhere. They wanted to starve the Israelis out. Maybe there was money to be made somewhere using that information.

He needed to place a phone call to Saudi Prince Rashid and tell him the good news. The Prince would be very pleased and the Prince paid very well. Vladimir toasted the Prince with another shot of vodka.

The winters in Moscow seemed to bother Vladimir the older he got and now he dreaded them completely. Maybe the Grand Caymans would be the perfect place to retire. It was warm, they had pretty women in bikinis, plenty of vodka and he could be close to all of his money. Yes, that was the place.

"Hello," came a voice on the other end of the line, bringing Vladimir's attention back to the cold confines of his Moscow office.

"Hello, good day Prince Rashid. This is—"

"I know who this is. Do you have good news for me or not?"

"Ya, the best. I have signed agreement with Westminster Petroleum and locked up all of the rigs that WP has idle for our Western project. This will deprive those pesky Israelis the ability to pump any oil, that's if they ever find any."

"Excellent! Very, very good my friend. There will be a large bonus in this for you. Very good work. I take it you have not read the papers of the past week, no?"

"No, I have not. I just returned to Moscow."

"Well, those stubborn Israelis have finally found a large gas and oil field off of their coast, in the field they call Leviathan. It appears to be one of the largest gas finds ever in the history of the Middle East. Bigger than anything we have here or that you have in Russia."

"What?" shouted an alarmed Varinsky. "I have not heard any of this. I need to speak to my staff about communications even when I am away on holiday."

"Well, the new find will make the Israelis completely energy self-sufficient for more than a hundred years," continued the Prince. "They also would have been able to compete with your country and mine to undercut our prices and drive the prices very low. But, only if they can pump and drill for the gas and oil. They won't be able to now, thanks to you, Vladimir."

"Ya!"

"Yes. It also means that if they had the WP drilling rigs they would be able to start drilling right away."

"Zat will not happen," said Vladimir, generously pouring another vodka for himself, "because if Sir Claude tries to break this agreement, we will tie him up in court for years."

"We too have our lawyers filing suit to claim that their drilling violates international agreements and property boundaries. It is frivolous but it will slow them down. But I must go now. Very good work, Vladimir. I knew I could count on you."

"Goodbye, Prince Rashid, it has been a pleasure doing business with you."

Vladimir danced a little jig at the thought of the huge bonus given to him by the Saudis.

It was now time for him to make his plans, he was going to defect to the Grand Caymans! They were to have an oil refining conference there soon and he would attend, falling too ill to return, needing medical attention. And then silently defect and obtain citizenship. It would be costly but just the cost of freedom was well worth it.

"Ya, that is vat I will do, I will retire to the Grand Caymans," he said, laughing out loud before stopping, his mind suddenly remembering listening ears are everywhere in modern Russia.

Chapter Twenty-Eight

Senator Abe Speigelman sat on the old leather sofa in his corner office in the Senate building, impatiently awaiting for a return phone call from the White House. He never waited with prior administrations and certainly not from a President in his own party. In the past all he had to do is merely have his assistant call the President's office and request a meeting, usually as he was putting on his suit jacket and leaving for the Oval Office. But not with this President.

The New York Senator's large wood paneled office was lined with citations, pictures and commendations from the last eight presidents but from this president he constantly felt he was being slighted. But that came with the territory of being a Senator. He would come around in time for the elections; all the Presidents usually did if they wanted to get re-elected. This President would be no different. He would come around. They all did, sooner or later.

His prized wall hanging was the crayon drawing from his three-year-old granddaughter, Rebecca. She was the apple of his eye, even though she had just learned to talk in complete sentences. She sounded like a politician already, just like her grandfather. He chuckled to himself. Maybe he could bring her to work someday when—

"Senator, sorry to disturb you but the White House just called and the President is available to see you now."

"Thank you, Claire." He didn't know what he would do without his loyal assistant and confidante when she retired next year to go back to New York and teach. He would change her mind somehow, he thought. He liked having her around. He donned his jacket and closed his briefcase, preparing to meet with the President, President Careb Hussein.

There was extra security everywhere, as the senior Senator from New York approached the President's office.

"I am afraid that I am going to have to ask you to open your briefcase, Senator. I am so sorry, Sir," said the young OPP Agent.

Feeling frustrated and being pressed for time, Speigelman blurted out, "This is the third checkpoint that I have had to go through, just to get inside the White House."

"I understand Senator but with the bombing of Director Galloway, the OPP is taking extra precautions. Also I am sorry we cannot allow cell phones or any electronic devices, including hearing aids, Senator."

"What? It is tough enough to hear with this damn contraption, let alone without it. This is an outrage."

From out of nowhere appeared Benjamin Cartwright who told his subordinate, the young OPP Agent, "It's okay, let him through. I will vouch for the security and moral integrity of Senator Speigelman."

"Thanks Ben. I appreciate it. I would be lost without my hearing aid."

"I am sure, Senator, but you can appreciate since the Deputy Director of The FBI was assassinated within such a close proximity to the President, the OPP is not taking any chances."

"Of course, of course, Ben, but really don't take yourself too seriously."

"But that's my job, Senator. I take all things seriously. Please follow me and I will show you to the President." Ben Cartwright, like Speigelman, was always upfront with him and never went back on his word, unlike some of the other Congressmen Cartwright had to deal with every day. He opened the door to the President's office and stepped aside, letting the long time Senator enter.

"Thanks for the help Ben," said the distinguished Senator.

"Anytime, Senator."

Speigelman entered the President's private office as the President remained seated behind his desk, poring over a report.

"Good morning, Mr. President."

"Good morning, Senator. My condolences for the loss of James Galloway, I know that the two of you were very close." He set aside the report he was reading and directed his full attention to the Senator.

"What can I do for you today, Senator? As you can imagine we are extremely busy mobilizing all of our resources to bring to justice the perpetrator of this terrible crime. I am meeting with the heads of all of the major American intelligence organizations within the next fifteen minutes to get an update on Director Galloway's assassination. Then I will be briefed by the British and French this afternoon. So my time is rather short."

"I appreciate you taking the time to see me, Mr. President, especially in these trying times, so I will be brief. I would like to offer the services of my committee, The Senate Committee on National Security, to help in the investigation. Past Presidents have found my services to be very helpful, Mr. President."

"Thank you, Senator, but I don't think that would be necessary." The President, impatiently stood, in a gesture to dismiss the Senator. "I think we have it well under control, and cannot imagine what the esteemed Senator's committee could possibly add to our investigation. But thank you so much for coming," said to the President to the still seated Senator.

"Mr. President, please just a few more minutes of your precious time, sir. Please."

"Yes, of course, Senator." The President sat back down, mumbling while checking his watch and clutching his reports.

"Mr. President, I had met with Director Galloway just a few days before his death. I had information from unnamed sources that greatly concerned me, which the FBI was already aware of and checking into."

"What was that, Senator?"

"That there was mole, a highly placed enemy mole, in the uppermost reaches of our government, bent on the destruction of our government and our way of life." He paused.

"During my discussion with the Director he stated, confidentially, that they had one of their operatives working on it and were close to unmasking that individual."

"A mole? A secret investigation without my knowledge? Did he say who was working on this project? Did he happen to say who he thought this supposed mole was in our government?" the president pressed.

"No, Mr. President, he did not. We were scheduled to meet again tomorrow for a further briefing but then came the assassination."

"Interesting, very interesting, Senator. I will certainly bring this information to the attention of those I will be meeting with this morning, to discuss in the fullest detail in the context of Director Galloway's death. Now, if there is nothing else, Senator, I really must be going, if you don't mind."

"Thank you for your time, Mr. President. However there is one other thing that Director Galloway mentioned."

"Yes, Senator," said an impatient President.

"He mentioned that although they did not know the identity of the mole, they did know the mission of the mole here in the United States."

"Yes, Senator, what is the role of the mole here, so to speak?" said the President, making fun of the serious subject brought to his attention by the Senator.

Brushing aside the sarcasm, the Senator continued, "Galloway felt that the mission of the mole was to weaken the United States financially. He further stated that the ultimate goal was the weakening of the United States so that our country would be unable to provide financial and military assistance to come to the aid and support of our ally, Israel."

"Senator, you have Israel on the mind."

"Mr. President, I have the well being of all democracies on my mind. I intend to support them in any way that I can, Mr. President. We do not want to be standing alone when the hordes of intruders come knocking on our door. Mr. President, may I be frank?"

"Please Senator, please do, by all means."

"Mr. President, you have not supported any of my initiatives or funding for the Israeli Government since you were elected to office. You have vetoed or cut all aid, military, financial and other programs that have helped to foster an independent Israel. At the same time, Mr. President, you are spending vast amounts of money, trillions upon trillions of dollars, money that we don't have, on pie in the sky projects, education initiatives, military, social programs and environmental projects that quite frankly, Mr. President, this country does not want or need. You are bankrupting this country and weakening it almost beyond repair, Sir."

"Senator Speigelman, you were elected by the good citizens of New York to represent them, I suggest you do just that and leave international affairs to the purview of the State Department and to the Office of the President. Thank you for sharing your views and opinions with me. Good day, Senator, I really must be going now."

Senator Abe Speigelman stood and faced a weary President and said, as he shook his hand, "Mr. President, this country was built on freedom and democracy, the same as Israel. The day that we as a country, turn our backs on the citizens of Israel, is the day we turn our back on our own freedoms. That will be a sorrowful day indeed. Good day, Mr. President, may God speed."

Chapter Twenty-Nine

The Vice President, John Alexander and Secretary of State, Winslow Howard, along with the other attendees were already assembled along the length of the boat shaped, antique cherry wood conference table, waiting for the President to arrive. The President entered at the rear of the meeting room and took his chair at the head of the table. The meeting was being held in the secure White House Situation Room, located in a sub-basement of the White House, three stories below the President's office.

At the President's direction they took their respective places, sitting in big leather black executive chairs and placed their briefing folders they had brought with them on the black pads in front of them. All folders were in red-marked folders with, *Highly Top Secret-* Advice To the President on the front and all were kept closed.

The American and Presidential flag framed the space behind the President's chair and the walls were flanked with large screen TVs, capable of picking up any television broadcasts from around the globe. The room was more silent than any other meeting government conference room, because of all of the sound deadening and anti-spying measures built into this most sensitive meeting room.

"Thank you for coming gentlemen," started the President. "Let's get down to business. I would like to hear from the CIA first and then an assessment from NSA, OPP and the DIA."

"Mr. President," said CIA Director Walter Thompson, "we have brought in for questioning an FBI cafeteria worker at the FBI who had access to Director Galloway's cell phone. After intense, non-stop questioning the man admitted to taking the Director's cell phone on one of his breaks while Director Galloway was in a meeting. He hid it in a bathroom in a restaurant in the District, where he returned later to retrieve it."

"Surveillance footage from cameras around the restaurant, show a hired international assassin leaving the place some fifteen minutes later. The assassin, who goes by the name of Jasara, is shown leaving the restaurant to parts unknown. We showed a number of photos to the hotel staff and found that he was the one who registered at the Watergate Hotel, room 7707 on the day of the bombing. He registered under an assumed identity. He left and has not been heard from or seen since. He has not been picked up by TSA at any airport or customs office."

"Mr. President, we have agents conducting a massive search for him but our scope is limited since our charter restricts us from performing operations in the continental United States. We will turn over all of our information to whoever will be the lead agency in this investigation."

OPP Director Cartwright spoke up to question Director Thompson, "Why would he leave such an open trail? Why would he make it so easy to find out about him? It makes no sense."

"Well sir, he is a professional but either he was paid so much money that now he just plans to hide for the rest of his life and was paid so much money he can afford to do so or..."

"Or what?"

"Either he is not done with his killings or he was directed to do so, so that it sends a message to us."

"What kind of message?"

"That anyone and everyone is vulnerable, Mr. Director."

The President interrupted, "Thank you Director Thompson. I think this Jasara fellow made that point perfectly clear when he blew Director Galloway's head off at the Kennedy Center. Now I would like to hear from the NSA."

Jack Drury stood and looked around the room before facing the President. "Mr. President, we conducted a massive search of telephonic communications around the time of Director Galloway's untimely death," he paused, pulled his glasses out of his suit jacket and began reading from his report.

"The call Director Galloway received at the time of his death was made using a throwaway phone." He searched through his paperwork, biding his time.

"Yes, Director Drury, we know that. What else do you have?"

"The call was initiated from the Watergate Hotel, room 7707, registered to a Mr. Rodney Storm—the same room Jasara checked into. Mr. Storm has been found on a fly fishing vacation in Canada and has now reported the passport either lost or stolen. We have determined that he has no connection to Director Galloway's death. We have also found that at the precise time of the murder there were a number of other calls placed and received by cells phones near Director Galloway."

The President leaned forward in his chair, pointing his finger directly at Drury saying, "You mean to tell me you can track down some bozo in Western Canada on fishing vacation in the wilds but you can't find some international assassin right here in D.C.? Give me a break, Mr. Director."

Drury stepped away from his seat, "We still have an extensive city search going on as we speak, Mr. President."

"Continue with your report, Director Drury," said a thoroughly disgusted President.

"Mr. President, it appears that Special Agent Nick Ryan, who was reported as being the last person seen talking to Jimmy, I mean Director Galloway, also received a call from his father in Florida. Agent Ryan also received a text message from a Delray Beach location in Florida."

"Who was the text message from, Director Drury?" asked Secretary of State, Howard.

"The text was sent by a Ms. Rosa Scalase."

"Oh God, don't tell me we have the mob involved in this shenanigans!" responded Secretary of State Howard.

"No sir, she is not connected at all with any crime syndicate, rather, she is an agent at the DEA and has checked out clean. However, we also found that at the precise time of the killing of Director Galloway there was a call made by Prince Yasim at the Kennedy Center to the Saudi Embassy. One minute later a call emanated from their embassy across the street from the Center to the Watergate Hotel, possibly to room 7707, 6584, 2390 or the front desk, we can't be sure at this point, Mr. President. We are still checking sir." He paused to let the gravity of the situation sink in.

He continued, "Gentlemen, it should be noted that it was Prince Yasim who led Director Galloway to the spot where he was killed. That spot is also in direct visual contact of the Watergate Hotel, room 7707."

"Continue, Director Drury," directed the President.

"Obviously we could not visit our friends at the Saudi Embassy and tell them we have been tracking and listening to all of their phone calls. But we also did trace a phone call from the Watergate back to the Embassy a few minutes later after the explosion, and are in the process of tracking it down from the hotel."

"Thank you, Director Drury. I don't think we can confront our friends the Saudis with this information until we are damn sure about our facts. Gentlemen get those facts, now! I do not want to keep you from pursuing this investigation with the greatest possible haste but I would like to take a moment to brief you on some recent intelligence I received from Senator Abraham Speigelman." He paused to look around the room before continuing.

"The Senator briefed me, just a few moments before coming to this meeting, that he had been informed just recently by Director Galloway about the discovery of an undercover mole, high within our government."

Shock registered on the faces of those in attendance at the meeting. There were rumors of the moles existence for the last three months throughout the agencies in attendance, but it had never been discussed so openly before that day.

"Gentlemen, I have reason to believe that this mole does indeed exist, but gentlemen, this is not to be discussed outside of this room. Please direct all intelligence on this matter that you receive to Director Cartwright and I ask that he continue the investigation under his direction. Thank you gentlemen for coming."

Chapter Thirty

The President stretched out his tall lanky frame on the sofa in the Oval Office, going over in his mind the meeting he'd just left. OPP Director, Benjamin Cartwright stood nearby waiting for the President's special instructions, which usually happened after he attended a meeting such as this.

"Ben, do you think there is a mole?"

"I don't know, Mr. President, but anything is possible, sir. I just don't know."

"Ben, I have to tell you, I spoke to Jim Galloway on the night he died, at the Kennedy Center. He told me of the existence of such a mole."

"He did, sir?"

"Yes, he did, but with great reluctance. He told me the mole was Nicholas Ryan. And even stranger, Ryan asked me for Galloway's job, he said, should anything ever happen to the Director. I thought it was rather peculiar at the time, him asking for the job should anything happen to Galloway and then within an hour Jimmy's head gets blown off. I don't believe in coincidences, do you Ben?"

"No sir, I do not."

"Ryan needs to be eliminated, quickly and quietly so that this information never comes to light. This nation cannot tolerate another shock to its system. The markets took a huge beating today as a result of Galloway's death. If there was even a leak about a mole it would be devastating to our economy. Do you understand me, Ben?"

"I am not sure exactly what you mean, sir."

"I am putting Ryan's name on our Prime Target List and designating him for immediate termination."

"You want him killed, sir?"

"Yes. I think it is best that this never comes out and it be handled quickly and personally, by you Ben."

"But, sir, I know Nick Ryan. He is a good agent. I can't believe he is a mole. Are you sure of your sources about this information, sir?"

"Yes, I am sure. That will be all, Ben. Call me when it is done."

"Yes, sir."

"And Ben, Galloway also told me Ryan was working on a special investigation. When you find him, bring everything he has to me?"

"Yes, Mr. President."

President Cerab Hussein waited until Cartwright left the room, before he walked over to the large mirror and tapped the bottom and the huge framed mirror swung out. He climbed the stairs and sat at his laptop while he connected to AlifMusic.com and connected, there he found all of the information he needed.

Later, he turned off his computer and went to his living quarters, sure that his wife Mary would be happy to see him early for a change. He would have dinner and await the phone call from Benjamin Franklin Cartwright. Tomorrow all of his problems would be solved.

• • •

Cartwright left the President's office torn but he knew what he had to do. He did not like it but he would do it nonetheless. He felt like he'd been hit by a truck, realizing that he had to take out a fellow Agent, a good agent in his mind but he always followed orders, always. Life was not always fair. Too bad about Nick Ryan. Now he was on his way, on his way to find Special Agent Nick Ryan. He would find him and he would kill him.

Chapter Thirty-One

The thunder rolled through Prince Rashid's palace in the desert. The rain and cooling air that came with it brought welcome relief to the hot, arid air in the desert kingdom. The Prince had taken refuge in the sands, refuge in the ways of the past where he and his entourage of fifty could hunt with his favorite falcons and luxuriate in the warm mineral springs in the cool evening of this oil rich nation.

The Prince had set in motion a series of events, conceived many decades earlier and had taken a lifetime to unfold, now spinning like a child's top, round and wobbly, spinning until it's final act and final spin. The genius and the audaciousness of the plan was only now becoming apparent as it spun its final spins.

Now there was only the loose ends to tidy up, for in his plan no loose ends could be left untied, all had to be disposed of before the final spin ended. After his call ended from his new partner in Russia, he placed the rest of his phone calls waiting for the final spin.

Prince Rashid called Alexander Smirnoff in Moscow to explain to him the wealth available for the enterprising spirit. He next called an old police contact in Baltimore to offer him a chance to retire earlier than he could ever imagine. The Prince's final telephone call was to a previous business acquaintance in New Jersey. He would make someone very happy today.

Finally Prince Rashid knew it was his day for sorrow, as he called Jarem, his most trusted bodyguard to his side.

"Jarem, I do not have much time left. Our mission is over and it will be a success. You have seen me through the many trials I have had to endure in order to complete my life's mission. I may not have much time left but there is something that must be done, something to tie up the final loose end. Something only you can do."

"Yes, Your Highness. Your wish is my desire."

"Forgive me my old friend for what I ask you to do, but it must be done."

"Yes, master. I understand. I will leave tonight."

"And Jarem, find Ishtar. Have my youngest son visit with me here."

"Yes Prince, as you wish."

The Prince was tired and his journey of life was nearing an end and looked out over the wide expanse of his kingdom. He pulled himself up to the cushions on the wide window ledge, where he could see his beloved desert for one last time.

His bright, youngest son, Ishtar had always been the most loyal and most cunning and would now soon be called upon to carry the burden of the kingdom on his broad shoulders. Ishtar had been educated both in the United States and in Great Britain at the finest schools available.

Ishtar was in his suite of rooms packing some clothes and belongings, preparing to go on his journey. Tall and handsome, dark hair and darker eyes, he was alluring to every woman he met, but he had little time or thought to entertain women. He had only one goal, the greater good of the kingdom.

The young prince excelled in math, engineering and computer sciences but always got into trouble when taking social sciences. He felt the world revolved around the greatest kingdom on earth, his homeland. Ishtar learned the Western ways and values and like his father thought of ways to use those ways to the kingdom's advantage.

He also saw something his father had taught him from the time he was a young child of the desert, the state of Israel was the root of all of the kingdom's problems. They both shared the vision that it should be eradicated from the face of the earth. But he would have to use all of his cunning in order to achieve his goal.

He never discussed his plans with his father but he felt today it was time to become a martyr for his cause. He was going to join the freedom fighters against the Americans and with others, drive them out of the Middle East. *This was their land and not the foreign Americans,* thought the young Prince.

His thoughts were interrupted by a knock on his door, it was Jarem.

"Prince Ishtar, your father would like to see you in his chambers."

"You have told him nothing of my quest, Jarem?" he said, his eyes heated with suspicion.

"No prince, while I do not agree with your journey and feel there are other ways to accomplish your ends, I am bound by my oath to you, not to say anything of your desires to your father."

"I leave tonight for my journey, Jarem."

"Prince your father is not well, perhaps a day or two wait is in order, my Prince."

"Jarem, do not dare to tell royalty about their mission. But I will give it some thought, careful thought."

"Yes, my Prince. Your father is waiting."

Prince Rashid's eyes brightened when he saw his youngest son enter his sleeping chambers, tall, straight, handsome and bright. He was so much like his father it made him proud. He approached his father and bowed slightly at the waist out of respect.

Prince Rashid patted the cushion next to him and motioned Ishtar to sit.

"You make me proud, my son. You are many things and I am proud of them all."

"Thank you father, but there is something I must tell you. Something I must do father."

"You are leaving, leaving this house to join the freedom fighters? No?"

Ishtar felt betrayed, betrayed by his closest confidant. *Jarem must have told my father.*

"I do not need Jarem to tell me what every fox in the desert already knows, my son. I will not try to stop you but I ask that you listen to what I have to say, listen one last time before you make your final decision."

"Yes, father." Ishtar settled in on the cushion next to the old man, the sun setting behind them.

"Years ago, my son, I embarked on a mission to destroy our enemy and the enemy of our entire world, Israel. I had seen where even with all of our armaments, our proud warriors, we could not drive them to the sea. They are too shrewd and they have powerful friends in key places in the world." The Prince began to cough and stopped talking to look at the sun dropping even lower on the horizon.

"I don't have much time, my son." The young prince moved closer.

"We tried armed conflict," his father continued, "wars, invasions, embargoes and even though our brave warriors tried to defeat them, the Americans were always there to help finance them and keep their country alive."

"Yes, that is so, father. But what can we do?"

We will defeat them using their own ways and do everything we can to keep Israel weak."

"What is that father?"

"We carefully recruited *Kitmans* from around the world, young, bright, energetic recruits who share our ideals and values. We trained them in our ways and sent them to return to their places of birth and become one of them again." He leaned towards his son rising on his elbows to make his point.

"My son, we sent the *Kitmans* back to America, England, Australia and all other places with strong ties to Israel. Their purpose was to weaken those countries by promoting large welfare programs, building armies, navies, giant social programs and anything that would sap their strength and energy. We also donated large sums of money to the environmental groups."

"Why environmental groups father?"

"My son we export our strength every day and every day we have less and less of our life blood, oil. We need to make sure that what little we have left lasts for a long time and we need to make sure that they do not discover any oil to make them less dependent on our oil. That is our only hope and survival. As long as we have oil, our way of life is strong and assured. The environmental groups are our best hope to ensure that America never drills for oil anywhere in the world or that it takes so much time it will be expensive to use. They have been our most effective tool, until now."

"I understand my father."

His father continued, "We need to make sure America is weak and cannot come to the support of our enemy, Israel. We also need to make sure that Israel never discovers oil, to make sure they are always weak. If they discover oil, which looks like it may be possible in the newest discovery they made, we need to make sure they never produce it, ever. We will tie up the drilling rigs, tie them up in court and any other way we can. Do you now understand, my son? Do you?" He grabbed the tunic of his youngest son.

"Yes, father I do now. But what can I do and why now?"

"You can take control and see this *Kitman* project through. We have and will have key people in power capable of moving this forward. But there must be someone here, as a Prince, to handle it."

"What about Prince Yasim? He is next in line, Father."

"He is not ready for this my son, he is weak in the Western ways. It is my fault for letting him live there among them for so long. But I will handle my mistakes, all of my mistakes."

The sun had now set behind him and the sound of the desert jackals could be heard howling in the distance.

"It is up to you my son, you, the new Prince. What say you, Prince Ishtar? Will you succeed your father and carry on as he has chosen for you?"

The Prince stood, straightened his tunic and knelt before his father saying, "Yes father I will defeat the Israelis and all of their minions, should you feel I am worthy."

The kneeling prince felt his father's hand on his head and heard him say, "Rise my Prince, the new heir to the kingdom."

The newly crowned Prince rose and went to show respect to his father, to embrace him. His father was facing the window and his beloved desert; it was the very last thing he saw before he died. Long live the new Prince, Prince Ishtar.

Chapter Thirty-Two

Nick made it across the lake and hitched a ride with a trucker back to Baltimore. He took a taxi back to the house he and Katie had shared, his home by the stream. He reflected on the death of Adrianna, those bullets were meant for him not her. He was sorry he ever got involved in the whole mess. Too many people were dying. He headed home.

To Nick, it seemed that every time he left his charmed little stone house, he was drawn back to the heartfelt place by the stream. But Florida was feeling more and more like home, Nick thought. It was a place where he could make a clean break and leave all of his disturbing memories behind him.

He opened the door and immediately went to the computer, fired it up and waited for it to go through its gyrations and long hello. The older he got the more impatient he became with the interminably long wait for the computer to start. If cars took this long to start up no one would ever get anywhere. Soon it was done with its machinations and Nick slipped the Digi-Tex flash drive into the USB port.

The computer whizzed and buzzed until finally the scene appeared on the screen. Nick watched as Krazir exhorted his legions of followers to go out and destroy America, go out and destroy civilizations.

What the hell did they ever build up, he wondered? They only wanted to destroy. What would they ever do if they got what they wanted? Then he remembered the slaughters perpetrated by the Taliban in Afghanistan. The degradations, the oppressive regimes that everyone thought they once wanted. Well maybe we should just let them have what they wanted. *Let them all go to hell,* he thought as he waded through the portions he had seen once before at the cabin.

The old man, Krazir, stood and greeted his followers as they walked, one by one in front of him, kissing his ring and bowing down before him. Nick watched as more than twenty stood in line to be blessed by him and bowing down to show their allegiance to this terrorist leader.

As the last one approached, he stepped forward to greet him personally with a large familial hug. He gripped the last one by the shoulders, waving to everyone and pointing to this one as someone special, someone very special. The younger man lowered his head and knelt down on one knee before Krazir to receive what looked like a special blessing.

The equally tall man finally stood, kissed Krazir's ring, hugged him like a brother and turned to leave. It was only then that Nick Ryan was able to see the face of the last man. His eyes betrayed him, it could not be. He paused the video, and replayed it in slow motion. He was right, his eyes had not deceived him, the man paying homage to Osama Krazir was a young Cerab Hussein, the current President of the United States.

He paused the video on the computer and froze the image to be able to examine it in greater detail. Hussein was younger then, but there was no denying it was President Cerab Hussein.

Nick now knew why everyone was dying. This was a secret that many people would kill to keep. Now he knew their secret. He had to let everyone know who was hiding in the Oval Office, but still stay alive. What was he going to do?

"How ya doin', Special Agent Ryan?" The voice came from the darker recesses of the room. The sound startled him. Nick knew he was a dead man now. He saw two figures walking slowly towards him from the shadows in the living room.

It was Detective Gaskins and his sidekick, Officer Leroy Jenkins, both with their police pistols drawn, pointing them directly at Nick Ryan.

"I thought I smelled dead fish in here. I should have known it was you Gandorf."

The smaller Jenkins landed a solid punch to Nick's midsection, doubling him over and sent him reeling to the stone floor of the house by the stream.

"Watch your mouth tough guy! That's Detective Sergeant Gaskins to you. Do you hear me?"

Ryan was still trying to catch his breath and could not answer him.

Jenkins kicked him hard in the stomach, asking him again, "You hear me boy?"

"Yeah, I hear you," Nick was finally able to say. His sides and ribs ached.

Gaskins sat down at the desk, glanced at the computer screen and looked down at Nick. "I knew all we had to do is wait around and you would come back here. You are so goddamn predictable, Nick, so predictable."

"Make yourself comfortable, Gandy," Nick said, trying to shift himself and sit up, without too much pain.

Gaskins shoved him down with his foot, "You stay right there where I can keep an eye on you, Agent Ryan."

Nick lay on the floor, looking up he spied his pistol strapped to the underside of the desk drawer. He looked over at Jenkins, who was sizing up the house to see if there was anything he wanted to steal and made a note that he was distracted.

"Jenky, keep your eyes on him. He is not just a pretty face. Don't trust him, keep your gun on him."

Jenkins, once alerted, shifted his pistol and pointed it at Nick, who was now leaning up against the old wooden desk.

"So what can I do for you, Detective?"

"Now that's more like it, Nick. Well, you see Jenkins and me came here to arrest you."

"Arrest me? On what charge?" Nick blurted out.

"Murder. We are going to arrest you on murder charges, Nicky boy," said Gaskins.

"Murder? This gets better as it goes along. Who am I supposed to have murdered? That's what I would like to know."

"Adriana Maheed. You shot her in the cabin by the lake and then set it on fire to destroy the evidence of your crime. Then you fled the scene of the crime. They will give you the needle for that Nicky my lad. The death penalty. That is if you ever stay alive that long."

"I had nothing to do with her murder, nothing at all. You got to believe me, Gandy. I cared for her. I would never kill her. Wait, how did you know about her death? It just happened."

Jenkins began to laugh.

"Oh, I believe you, Nick. I believe you had nothing to do with her murder. Truly I do," Gaskins said looking at Jenkins. "I know because Jenkins here shot her, thinking it was you."

"Yeah, yeah, yeah, Nicky my boy. I thought it was you coming out of the cabin. I saw your outline clear as day, even at night in my sniper scope, wearing that red jacket and all, ha, ha, ha. I got three shots into her before she even hit the ground. Damn am I a good shot! We got paid a lot of money by some rich Arab prince to take you both out. Now we'll just pin the murder on you. "

Nick's fury boiled over, as he leaped to the throat of the man who slaughtered Adriana right before his eyes. Nick was tripped by Gaskins on his way to wreak havoc on Jenkins, tumbling to the floor.

"Hold it right there, Nick," said Gaskins cocking his pistol and training it at Nick's forehead. "Don't make me shoot you before your time. But that's not the end of it, you see you're also wanted for killing a police officer." Jenkins rolled and laughed all the more at Nick's expense.

"What? What do you mean? What police officer? I have never shot a cop! Never."

"Well, Nick there is always a first time."

"Who did I shoot?"

"You murdered a Patrolman. You shot Officer Leroy Jenkins, that's who." Jenkins continued to laugh at Nick, until he suddenly turned to look at his best friend Gaskins. Gaskins pulled the trigger of his thirty-eight caliber colt pistol and put a slug into the forehead of the dumb cop. The laughing stopped.

"He had a big mouth. Never did like that guy," said Gaskins, instantly retraining his pistol on Nick. Gaskins backed away from him, walking towards the door.

"There was a struggle and you shot Jenkins and then I shot you. Sorry Nick, but that is the way it has to be. Bye comrade," he raised the pistol and pointed it right at Nick.

Nick jumped and rolled over the ground in front of the desk and grabbed the .45 from its location under the desk drawer, pulling the trigger. The gun fired with the sound reverberating throughout the small cottage. The bullet hit Gaskin's left arm, just below the shoulder. He let out a yelp of pain but Gaskins pistol was still trained on Nick. Gaskins grimaced from the gunshot, as the blood trickled down his arm and started to pool on the floor.

"Damn that hurts, Nick. You should not have done that. I was going to be kind to you and give you one quick one in the skull but now I am going to have to make it hurt. Bye-bye Nicky boy."

Gaskins raised his gun and Nick heard the loud crack of a pistol firing, the sound exploded in the cabin. The old cop stood there with his crooked smile frozen on his face. He dropped, face forward and landed at Nick's feet. Nick's mouth fell open at the sight of Ben Cartwright standing behind Gaskins, his pistol still in his hand, the smoke of the gunpowder curling in front of his drawn revolver.

"That was close," said Cartwright, still holding his pistol pointed at Nick. "That bullet was supposed to have your name on it Ryan," he said walking towards Nick. He returned his weapon back into his underarm holster and went to check on Jenkins and Gaskins.

"They're both dead," he told Nick. "They have been doing some contract hits for the last couple of weeks for some big money guy in the Middle East, just don't know for who."

"Well, you came in just the nick of time, no pun intended," said Nick.

Ben stared at the computer screen. "So this is the chip that everyone has been searching for and dying for?"

"Yeah, Ben, this is it. You won't believe what is on it."

"I can well imagine. Let me guess," said Cartwright, pulling a chair near Nick. "It confirms that the President of The United States, Cerab Hussein, is the high level undercover mole or *Kitman* as they called him, sent here to wreak havoc on our country. Hussein sent me here to kill you, Nick, to keep the contents of this chip a secret and keep it quiet and he probably is lining up someone to kill me to cover the whole thing up. That's the way they like to work, no loose ends. They just kill everybody."

"You knew?"

"Of course we knew he was at least one of the moles planted in our government. We are close to finding the second mole but could not prove Hussein was the first. At least not until now. I was sent under deep cover from the FBI to work for the OPP. It just so happens that Hussein took a liking to me and promoted me to head up the OPP. We kept tabs on him but his spending went viral and out of control. His goal is to spend this country into bankruptcy. There was nothing we could do but just watch and bide our time."

"Well, he is doing a good job at one thing I guess, bankrupting our country," said Nick in a half laugh.

"His backers overseas are pulling his strings and directing everything he does."

"How does he communicate with them?"

"We think he would log onto an overseas website and download music onto his MP3 player and the instructions are in the song's lyrics. That's what led us in this direction. We were told that those of his belief abhor music. That was the key."

"Good work," said Nick.

"But other things such as his financing of his education, his trips abroad to Pakistan and his disappearances at crucial times, is when we discovered he was meeting with his handlers overseas. He is a very bright and wily foe, do not underestimate him."

"Yeah, I know."

"The problem is what do we do with the chip and the evidence that is on it? The President wants me to turn it over to him or to the FBI. If I do this I will meet an untimely death. His secret would then be safe. He has others working for him strategically placed in the government. This country means too much to me. I can't let that happen, Nick. But there is nothing we can do," said the dejected Cartwright.

"Not necessarily," said Nick, turning his gaze to the nearby laptop. "The Internet is an awesome weapon, but only if you know how to use it properly. I think I have our answer, Ben."

Chapter Thirty-Three

The video went viral as soon as it hit the Internet, leaked by Wiki-Leaks and picked up by dozens of other similar sites around the globe. It caught mainstream media completely off guard, as it spanned the globe, soon becoming the number one story by breakfast time in Washington D.C.

The President immediately issued a denial saying the video was a fraud perpetrated by his political opponents. Still the clamor across the country rose to a fever pitch for an investigation or his resignation and like a Tsunami, the problems could not be pushed aside.

President Hussein issued more denials but nothing could stop the call for him to step aside, even while the video was investigated. By that afternoon it was the only story that was of any importance and received continuous coverage by every network worldwide, both large and small.

The death blow for the President came late that same afternoon when the FBI proclaimed that using sophisticated electronic measuring equipment; they were able to verify that the video was real and not a fraud. The President addressed the nation that evening on national television.

"Good evening, my fellow Americans. I am sure by this time you have all either seen or heard of the video circulating on the Internet and television waves across this great nation of ours. It purports to show a figure, altered to look like me, paying homage to one of the most vilified people on this planet, Osama Krazir.

"I come before you tonight to say that this is not only completely untrue but a patent forgery of someone made to look like me.

However due to this storm of criticism and distrust it has made it impossible for me to lead this great nation.

"Therefore at 8:00 o'clock tonight, Washington time, I will effectively turn over control of this government, in keeping with our constitution, to Vice President Alexander.

"It is unfortunate that this distraction has come at such a crucial time in our nation's history. After discussions with my family and with my cabinet advisors, and the deepest soul searching, I find this is the best course of action both for me and my family and for this great country."

"I ask that everyone please give their complete support to your new President, John Alexander and his programs. I assure you that the new President will continue to pursue the programs that I have started and with your help will bring this great nation into its promised prosperity. Thank you ladies and gentlemen for your time and patience during these troubled times. God bless America."

The nation could not believe what they were hearing. Their President was resigning! They now would have a new President, one unknown to most of the country. It would take a long time for the new name to become an everyday word, President John Alexander.

Alexander had been chosen to pull the votes from the conservatives and from those interests out West. He championed the Silent Majority and the Neo-Conservatives of the right. All of the strategies had worked to get Hussein elected President. John Alexander would now be President. The nation held its collective breath to see what kind of President he would be, and how he would lead.

Chapter Thirty-Four

"Are you coming to bed, dear? I mean are you coming to bed, Mr. President?"

"I'll be there in a bit, sweetheart. Tomorrow is a big day and I must be totally prepared. You understand don't you, dear?"

"Of course, John, I understand. I am so looking forward to tomorrow when the Chief Justice swears you in. I am so excited I can hardly wait. I know I won't be able to sleep without my little round pill."

"I will see you in the morning, dear. Don't worry, I will wake you, so you don't miss a thing, I promise."

"I love you, John."

"I love you too, Margaret. Now get your rest. I'll see you in the morning."

John Alexander walked from the large bedroom to his new office, his steps muffled by the thick cream carpet. The ever present Secret Service agents shadowed him at a discreet distance. The lead agent, Phil Muth, spoke into his communications device, secured inside his jacket sleeve, alerting others, "POTUS is on the move," and they all swung into action.

Alexander reflected back on his rise to the pinnacle of power in the United States. He had gone from city councilman, to mayor of Cody, Wyoming, to state Senator, to U.S. Congressman, to Senator to Vice President.

He was always in the background, but always effective, always working for change. Now the biggest change in American government was about to take place in the United States and no one knew anything about it.

It had been so easy. Tomorrow he would be sworn in as the next President of the United States. He was overcome with joy and anticipation. The plan was working, he would be the next President and Careb Hussein was now on his way back to his home state of Puerto Rico in disgrace.

Careb had been so dumb, and so susceptible. He got caught. Everyone thought him to be the only spy, the mole. *Ha, ha, ha, ha,* Jack had to laugh. Now everything was going just as the Prince had told him it would go, just as he had planned it. He paid homage to the all knowing Prince Rashid.

He laughed out loud to himself and quickly put his fist to his lips to prevent himself from being heard. *So easy,* he thought, as he massaged the red crescent star on his wrist, *so easy.* He had them convinced that poor Careb Hussein was the only *Kitman.* He nearly wept at their stupidity. Hussein had no idea what happened to him but Alexander knew that the Prince's plan had worked beautifully.

President Alexander looked out over Pennsylvania Avenue and watched all of the activity awaiting his first day in office. They were building the platforms for his speech and the parade would march right in front of his oval office. All he had been waiting for, was for someone to connect the dots and all of the dots pointed to Careb Hussein as the only *Kitman.* He laughed at the amusing turn of events.

Tomorrow his fight for justice against the infidels would begin in earnest. But he must use his cunning and his intellect and all of his friends in Congress. Nothing could stop him now that Careb had been moved out of the way. The non-believers would pay for all of their injustices to the chosen ones. Tomorrow was the day, the beginning. He had fooled them all.

Chapter Thirty-Five

Nick picked his father up at Dulles Airport and they drove together in silence towards the Grande Hotel.

"I am so sorry about Adriana, Nick," said his father, breaking the bond of silence as they drove through the D.C. suburbs on the Dulles Access Road, past the endless subdivisions of homes outside of Washington. Working class homes dotted the countryside, with large lawns. The newly planted trees all backing up against the highway, seemed pushed together like sardines in a can which made for the perfect backdrop on a day like today.

Everyday life was moving on, lawns still needed to be cut, kids needed to be taken to school and the newspaper was delivered on the front porch, just like the day before. Life had not really changed. Life goes on.

"I did not know her long, Pop, but she was a really good person. She was exciting, she was different. But I have learned a lot since I saw you last."

"Yes, son? Tell me, what have you learned?"

"Life goes on and sometimes when you least expect it, someone or something knocks on your door and you have a choice, you can answer or you can ignore it. But ignore it at your own peril. I will not let that happen to me again, ever. I want to live life again so when I get back to Florida I want to try to make amends with Rosa, if she'll let me."

"Good. Makes an old man feel good, Nick. Welcome back to the human race."

"It's good to be back, Pop."

"I understand you ran into Tripp and our old friend, Ben Cartwright?"

"Yes, I did. Cartwright saved my life and Tripp, well you know Tripp. Tripp is Tripp. Maybe we can get together with him and have a beer?"

"That would be great."

"This city never changes," remarked his father, as they drove through downtown from stoplight to stoplight, with the endless stream of tourists filling the crosswalks in center of D.C. stopping in front, all of them marveling at the nation's capital.

"No, it never does and never will."

"What time is the funeral?"

"Jimmy's funeral service is at two o'clock tomorrow. He requested a small ceremony at Arlington National, no church, only words at the gravesite. You know Jimmy, nothing fancy. Today they have the swearing in ceremony for President Alexander. Go figure who would have ever thought."

"Hell, I was surprised when Hussein chose the guy as his Vice Presidential running mate. And from Wyoming of all places."

"Yeah, go figure. I got us two adjoining rooms Pop and after we check in, we can go out and get something to eat or just order in room service. Whatever you like."

"Room service sounds good. We can watch the swearing in ceremony on TV, eat something, then I can whip your butt in a game of chess."

"Sounds great," said Nick as they swung their car in front of the Grand Hotel and left the car for the valet.

Nick changed into the clothes his father had brought him from his apartment. It was good to be wearing his own clothes again. He heard a knock on the door, and as he opened a young girl wheeled in a cart filled with food.

"Your room service order, Mr. Ryan," she said, smiling as she handed him the check and lifted the silver domed covers off of the food meant to keep the food warm. "Steaks, with onions, and French fries," she said. Nick laughed, *his father would never change.*

"Thank you."

Nick and his father watched the swearing in ceremony of the new President as they ate.

"I never have seen anything like this in my life, at least not since Nixon," said his father.

"Yeah," said Nick, watching the new President very closely. *Something very familiar about him,* Nick thought, very familiar.

The next morning they went down for breakfast and afterwards walked around the city before having to head back to the hotel to prepare for the funeral. The Capital sidewalks were jammed with government workers scurrying for a quick lunch and rushing in between the army of tourists taking pictures of everything they saw.

The sidewalks in Washington were wide. Wide enough to drive a car on but regardless of how wide they made them, they were always full.

"Look Pop, the forsythias are in bloom," Nick remarked.

"Yeah son, that they are," his father said, smiling, glad to have his son back with him again. He had not noticed flowers since Katie died. She had loved flowers.

The service was small, by Galloway's request, but he still received full honors, including his casket being carried by the Army's elite Honor Guard, the same guards that tend the flame at the Tomb of the Unknown Soldier. Jimmy always admired them and their dedication and because of his years of military and government service, he was buried in the field of honor at Arlington National.

The Honor Guards uniforms were impeccable, without a visible wrinkle from head to toe in their bright blue wool pants with the streaming gold stripe. The visors on their caps shined to a high gloss to match that of their shoes and above the visor was the smallest ring of gold at the top of the rim of the cap.

At the graveyard, the minister from Jimmy's non-denominational church, said just a few short words about Jimmy before blessing the casket. Jimmy had left the Catholic Church years ago over a disagreement his wife had many years before with the church but he secretly went to mass every weekend without her knowledge.

Standing across from them was Ben Cartwright, the new Director of the FBI. His immediate promotion had been pushed by the Congressional Oversight Committee with the blessing of the new President. Standing beside the FBI Director was his newest Assistant Director, Tripp Jackson. Nick smiled when he saw Tripp and was pleased about his promotion.

The minister finished just in time for the rain to start pouring down on the assembled crowd.

"Goodbye, Jimmy," said Nick as he touched the casket with the raindrops now dribbling in streams of water down the side. "You'll be missed."

"That he will be," said his father. "Let's go have a toast to Jimmy, one for the road he will travel."

Ben Cartwright came over and shook both Nick and his father's hand. "How you doing, Frank? Good to see you up and about. How the hell you been?"

"I'm good, Ben. Real good. Thanks for saving the life of my boy here."

"The least I could do," he said, turning his attention to Nick. "Nick I could really use you back at the agency. Take some more time, get your affairs in order and come to Washington and join us here. What do you say?"

"Sounds like a tempting offer, let me sleep on it okay?"

"Take as much time as you need, just don't wait too long Nick. Frank good to see you again but I'm sorry I got to go, new job and all. Think about it and let me know Nick, so long."

Tripp came over and gave Frank Ryan a hug and shook Nick's hand vigorously. "Look what it takes to get us all here together. Let's go have a beer and toast Jimmy, my treat."

O'Neill's Pub, a small bar off of K Street, looked more American than Irish but their saving grace was that they had Guinness beer on tap. It was the drink of gold for the Irish, the drink that made leprechauns taller and the perfect way to celebrate the life of one so dear.

The dark stout beer, dribbled down the inside of the beer glass. It turned brown when it reached the bottom and slowly changed to black as it settled and froth rose and then, and only then, could it be drunk by the Irish faithful.

"Here's to Jimmy," toasted Frank Ryan. "Goddamn, he should have been here. It just doesn't feel right without him."

"Here's to Jimmy," the other two chimed in. They talked and drank, drank and talked for a couple of hours before ordering corned beef and cabbage from the bar. The meal was excellent and appropriate for the occasion.

"Congratulations on your promotion," said Nick when his father went to relieve himself in the men's room.

"Yeah. I have worked with Ben off and on for a number of years and he told me to stop being a vagabond and settle down with one government agency. Make a home and put down some roots. So what the hell, I'll try anything. What about you?"

"Well, I do have to say it sounds tempting but I'll just have to see what happens."

"All right, all right you two, enough of this dribble. Let's eat and then I have to head back to the hotel. I can't miss my *Wheel of Fortune* show."

"Pop, you can't be serious."

"You bet I'm serious, dead serious. Come on drink up. Oh and Nick I got a call from my brother in Alaska and he said to say hi. He's going to try to come down to visit us in Delray. It will be great."

"Yeah great," Nick whispered under his breath at the thought of his long lost uncle staying with him. *Just great.*

Chapter Thirty-Six

Jasara did not like being a sitting duck in the hotel and now regretted agreeing to cool off at the Grande for a couple of days after the assassination. His biggest advantage was his mobility. As long as he was on the move after a hit he could blend in anywhere. He did not like being cooped up in a hotel, waiting for his bonus and final name on his list.

Carlos had the worst headache ever standing outside of Jasara's room. He'd seen the man in his vision, sitting in a room, wearing green pajamas along with the hotels white robe. His pistol was tucked in the rear of his pajamas bottoms. Carlos massaged his temples, trying to ease the pain until finally the headache went away. He pushed the service cart in front of him.

There was a knock at Jasara's hotel room door.

"Room service," came the cheery call. He opened the door and a cart was pushed in by a dark haired man wearing a white server's jacket.

"Where's Becky? She's the one who normally brings me my breakfast," said Jasara sitting in a room, wearing a green pajamas and the hotel's white robe.

"She is off today, sir," said the waiter, locking the wheels to the cart and pouring orange juice from a large cold container on the cart. "Fresh squeezed," said the waiter, handing the chilled glass to him.

Jasara tied a napkin around his neck, his mouth watered for the ham and cheese omelet he had grown accustomed to eating since his stay at the Grande. The waiter removed the silver domes covering the plate and pointed a Walther PPK 7.65 mm pistol with silencer off it directly at Jasara's head.

The first bullet entered the skull in the center of the forehead before Jasara could even register its existence. The second bullet was not even necessary because the lights had already been turned out in his head and Jasara slumped over dead in his chair, the white napkin still draped around his neck, with splatters of blood dripping down the center.

To Jasara, everything happened in slow motion. He had seen the barrel of the silencer pointed at his head and saw the flash of light. He saw the bullet coming at him slow enough he thought he could see the barrel markings on the projectile, until he felt the searing pain in his forehead, entering his skull and then he saw nothing.

Carlos Scarlatti, returned the silver domes to cover the plates and pushed the cart outside of the room, down the hallway and into a service area. He threw the pistol, the waiter's jacket and his gloves down the elevator service shaft and headed up the three flights of stairs to his room.

The New Jersey hit man picked up his bag and headed for the taxi stand. He was done. He was going to retire. He had been in Washington D.C. for too long and it was too close for comfort to his friend in New Jersey. It was dangerous to stay any longer. He left his room, closing the door behind him. Next door a sweet young thing with a short skirt, long brown hair and fantastic body was having trouble getting into her room.

"Damn thing won't work," she muttered under her breath as Carlos passed behind her. He stopped, looking at her shapely figure and how it nicely filled out her clingy skirt. *Worth a shot*, he chuckled at the pun.

"Just knock and your husband will let you in," he said in passing by her.

"No he won't, he's in Los Angeles. Can you help me, it just won't open."

Carlos stopped and looked at her. She was real sweet looking thing and seemed to be just his type.

"I would really appreciate it," she said with a come hither smile.

"Sure, I have a minute. Let me take a whack at it." He took the electronic card from her hand and swiped it, the green light came on immediately and the door clicked open. "There you go. You must have had the swipe portion backwards."

She kissed him on the lips, hard. "Do you have a minute for a proper thank you?"

"I'll make time," said Carlos, following behind her, his eyes fixated on her sexy, gentle swaying. When he walked in the room there were six weapons trained on him, it was his old buddies from New Jersey. These guys were not messing around, he knew if he twitched, he was a dead man.

George "Big Gumbo" handed the young girl a fat envelope and as she left he said, "Thanks sweetheart, you done good, real good," before turning his attention to Carlos.

They called him Big Gumbo because he originally came from Louisiana and all he ever wanted to eat was gumbo soup and at three-hundred-fifty pounds he ate whatever he wanted.

"Well, well, lookie here," said Big George in mock surprise. "What do we have here? Is that Carlos, the great lover and hit man, Carlos Scarlatti? What do you know? Good to see you again, Carlos. We been lookin' for you, lookin' for a long time," said the huge man.

The big man stood up and faced Carlos. "Mr. Romano has a burning desire to sit down and talk with you, Carlos. A real burning desire. You know what he does in his spare time now don't you? He uses a blowtorch to take apart cars and I know that he would love to turn that blowtorch on you and take you apart." He laughed so hard, his stomach bounced up and down over his white belt.

"Come on boys, tie his hands behind him, and we'll go down the back stairs." Carlos felt a sharp pinch at the back of his neck, like a bug bite and then his eyes became glossy and foggy before he passed out on the floor. "No need to take any chances and let him get away," said Big Gumbo.

Carlos Scarlatti made the trip to New Jersey in the trunk of a big black Cadillac and the handsome, dark haired lover boy was never seen again.

Chapter Thirty-Seven

Vladimir Varinsky began to make his plans. He was finished with Russia and its cold weather and shortages of most items in the stores. When even toilet paper is short listed it was time to go. Even though he was in the upper reaches of the Russian hierarchy, he was fed up. He was going to make his move to the Grand Caymans.

He sent his Ukrainian girlfriend Rackei back home to the Ukraine so she could visit her parents. He promised her he would come for her in a few weeks as he envisioned the warm beaches, the hot bikinis and the healthy salt air.

He had made his arrangements to ensure that he could easily access his money once he got to the Caymans and he was set.

"Slvetna," he called to his Secretary over his antiquated intercom system, "Slvetna? Can you call my car around please. I am late, I must go to the airport."

"Yes, Commissar Varinsky. I will do it right away. It will be downstairs waiting for you."

"Thank you, Slvetna." He never thought about leaving her any money because he never trusted her and she would just betray him anyway. His chauffeur Karlov, was another matter but he still had the same issue. If anyone suspected he was going to defect, then they would all be dead, including himself or he would just disappear and never been seen again courtesy of the secret police. So it was best just to leave quietly.

Karlov drove the Zil limo in front of the large grey nondescript building. He placed the luggage in the trunk of the Russian automotive behemoth while Vladimir kept his small briefcase with him. It contained everything he needed to access his offshore wealth.

Vladmir was as giddy as a schoolgirl as he rode to the airport, barely able to contain his excitement. He opened a bottle of his favorite vodka, added three ice cubes to a glass and poured himself a drink. He was on his way.

Krachinko was a small private Moscow airport on the outskirts of the city, used only by senior government and high ranking corporate officials. The small airport was deserted at this time of night and the limo pulled to the rear of the hangar, between two corporate jets. *This is it!* He finished a sip of his drink as the car glided to a complete stop.

Karlov, opened the rear door of the limo and helped Vladimir out of the car, securing his briefcase and helping him onto the plane. The driver buckled his nearly unconscious boss into the big tan leather seat at the rear of the jet and told the pilot everything was secure.

The drugs in the vodka worked quickly and effectively and Vladimir Varinsky would sleep the entire six hour flight to Permusk in Eastern Siberia, the coldest city in Russia. He would awake with no identification papers, no wallet, and no money aboard a stolen plane. He would be there a very, very long time.

The chauffeur, Karlov hugged his new girlfriend Slvetna and fondled the briefcase with the greatest affection, as they boarded the other jet to the Grand Caymans.

"You are so smart, Karlov," Slvetna said to her lover.

"No, my love, he was just so dumb and so greedy. Toast to modern capitalism," he said as the sleek gold and white jet lifted high above the skies over Moscow.

Chapter Thirty-Eight

The boat rocked and dipped like a roller coaster on the untamed waters in the Mediterranean far off the coast of Israel. The water breached the side of the ship flooding the decks from side to side. John Nagle had seen rough weather but none as rough as this.

He was on his way to shore to meet a courier sent to him by Sir Claude. But what did it matter now? He needed a commitment on those drilling rigs now, not two weeks from now. The battered boat finally reached port and was tied up at the pier when the skies opened up and it began to pour.

What else was he going to face today? Who was the courier? And why? Then it struck him, the courier was delivering the final termination agreements for the rigs. He had heard about the Russian deal with WP and their drilling rigs. He was sunk. Those Brit's always wanted all the T's crossed and their I's dotted, all legal like. Hey, he had a good run and he would come back even stronger. Hell, who was he kidding?

The door to the field office blew open and there sitting at his desk was Chelsea, Chelsea Borders.

"Hoy," said Nagle to her, so happy to see her now, he even forgot about his problems.

"Hoy," she replied in typical English Cockney fashion. They stood there appraising each other, not saying a word, their thoughts speaking volumes. He had been thinking about her a lot since he had left London. He missed her and every time he had to leave her he missed her even more. Something in the way she now looked at him told him the answer to the question he always asked himself.

God she looked good today. What the hell, he had been married once and life was good for him then, why not give it another try even though he would be broke soon? He would have to tell her everything.

It was he who spoke first, "I am so glad to see you Chels, you have no idea."

"Oh, yes I do," she said taking a step closer. She loved this crazy American, with his wild Texas ways, the gaudy cowboy boots and the big oval silver belt buckles he always fancied. God did she miss him when he was away from her. She had never been married but somehow it suddenly had an appeal to her.

The office staff watched this tango of love progress.

"It was not until this very moment that I realized how much I truly care for you, Chels," explained John Nagle. "I love you."

"I love you too, Johnny. I always have, but you know that, don't you?"

"Yes."

They met in the center of the office in a wild embrace, their lips searching for each other fueling the flames. They kissed the long kiss that had been missing in both of their lives. It was a different kiss, a kiss of love.

"Get a room," came an anonymous comment from somewhere deep in the office.

They both laughed like school kids and John showed her into his temporary office.

"It is so good to see you. You are not the courier from Sir Claude are you?"

"Yes. And I bring news. The board asked for Sir Claude to resign from the company and the board. It is not public knowledge but he has already agreed to do so. He says he wants to be an oil man again, whatever that means."

"Yes, go on Chels," said Nagle, hardly able to keep his hands off of her.

"At the board's request Sir Claude was selling off assets to any buyer who could come up with cash. The Third American Bank of Texas had seized all of the rigs off the US coast after the Deepwater

Sunset debacle. They had no use for them so he negotiated with the bank to buy them for his new private company, CJC."

"What the hell does that stand for?"

"Well it will stand for Claude, John & Chelsea, Inc. once you sign these papers."

"Where did he get the money to buy these rigs? Even discounted they are expensive."

"Sir Claude went to the Chinese and they are willing to put up the money to buy some of your natural gas here in Israel and become a steady customer, but they don't have a need for any drilling rigs."

"Wow, all of our problems are solved."

"Not all your problems, Johnny."

"What's left?"

"There is one stipulation that Sir Claude wanted but I told him you would never go for."

"What's that?"

"He said he would not consider doing any of this unless you and I got married."

"Tough question, but he needn't had bothered. I love you, Chels, always have. Will you marry me?"

"Yes." They embraced and the outside room clapped and cheered until John lowered the blinds and they were well hidden from view.

Chapter Thirty-Nine

The royal family jet left the Jeddah airport winging its way to the United States. It was not the usual journey that Jarem, the Prince's most trusted bodyguard, would take, for on this day he was alone.

The Prince was not with him and this was a journey Jarem was taking with a heavy heart. His Master had given him the ruby red signet ring, with a red star crescent chiseled on the front. He was acting as an emissary of the Prince. He was on his way to see the Crown Prince Yasim. His Master felt that the Crown Prince was not ready and would serve his followers more pain then they deserved.

The plane landed and was met by an entourage of vehicles, befitting an emissary from their Prince. Nowhere to be seen was Crown Prince Yasim.

Jarem had nurtured the young prince from the cradle onward. He had taught him to kill the wild boars in the huge thickets near the rivers and how to train the desert hawks to hunt. Jarem had taught how to ride the wild Arabian stallions and where to seek shelter and water under the hot desert sun.

But most of all he tried to teach him respect and obedience for his elders. Those were lessons not well learned, thought Jarem as the entourage made its way through the bustling capital of the Western world. Crown Prince Yasim had been under its spell for too long.

The long fleet of white limos pulled into the sprawling Saudi Embassy compound near the river and the drivers immediately disembarked to open the door for Emissary Jarem.

He was greeted at the entrance gate by the Consular Jasmud, "*Assalamu' alikum*."

"And peace be with you," responded Jarem. "I need to see Crown Prince Yasim."

"He is not here at the moment, Emissary."

"Where is he?"

"He is out with his American friends at the nightclubs. But he is a very good boy, Emissary."

"On your life's honor, who is he with and what is he doing?"

The consulate knew when this was invoked and he was approached in this manner, to lie would mean certain death.

"He is with some young American girls and they are dancing and drinking."

"Go now and when he returns bring him to me in my room. That is all."

The compound was soon deserted except for the guards and their guard dogs patrolling to insure tranquility and no idle curiosity seekers. At five a.m. a drunken Crown Prince Yasim was shown to the room of Jarem.

The Emissary Jarem was solemn and very quiet. "Where have you been, Yasim?"

"You have no right to ask me that. Just because you knew me when I was young does not give you the right to speak to me in that manner. Only my father can speak to me in that manner."

"Where have you been, Yasim?" he repeated.

"Out, if you must know. I was out drinking and dancing."

"Those are not our ways, Yasim."

"Well our ways must change, Jarem. This is the new way of the world."

"We have prospered for centuries with our ways. And we will continue to prosper abiding by our ways."

"How dare you talk to me like that? You are just an employee of my father's."

Jarem showed him the signet ring with the red crescent star. "I am an Emissary of your father. He is concerned about you and your new lifestyle in America. He is concerned if you are fit to lead our people or should your younger brother be the next leader?"

"That is my birthright not my brother's. I want to talk to my father." He stood to leave the room, now blocked by Jarem.

"That is not possible," said Jarem.

"What do you mean, not possible? Out of my way stable boy."

"Your father died while you were out engaging your wild Western ways. He felt you are incapable of leading and that your younger brother Ishtar should be appointed in your place."

"He cannot lead my people as long as I am alive," shouted Yasim, pushing his way past Jarem.

"Yes, that is true my Prince."

Yasim did not see the dagger come from within the folds of Jarem's flowing white robe, the dagger so sharp he did not at first feel the thrust of it through his stomach. The blood rushed to his mouth from his wound and the surprised look on his face soon faded as he slipped to the carpet covering the floor below.

Crown Prince Yasim gasped for air. Jarem placed a pillow beneath his prince's head until his eyes finally closed. Jarem then turned the dagger on himself and after three methodical stabs, he lay next to his Prince, his white robe slowly turning the brilliant color of crimson.

The official account of the deaths was reported in the country's main publication. No police were allowed into the compound to confirm or deny the embassy's account of the deaths. They had to take the word of the new Prince, Prince Ishtar. The newspapers the next day would proclaim that both the Prince and his father's trusted body guard had committed suicide after learning of Prince Rashid's death. Both bodies were returned to their native land for a burial fit for a king.

Chapter Forty

It was good to finally be back in Florida, *home*, thought Nick, as Southwest Airlines flight #687, landed then taxied to the terminal. This is home now. Nick looked out the window of the plane and thought of Adriana and the time they had spent together, her smile, her sense of humor and her sense of wonderment. His mind flashed with the thought of her laying there on the floor of the cabin, dead. He missed her.

He woke his snoring father from a sound sleep. It had been a long day for him.

"We home already?" he questioned.

"Yeah, Pop, we're home. Come on, let me get you back to Stephens and then I am going to finally get some shut eye."

"I still can't believe Jimmy is gone," moaned Nick's father. "He was such a good friend. It would be like losing you Nick."

"Now don't get all sentimental on me, Pop."

"Oh, you know what I mean."

They made their way out of the baggage terminal to the parking garage where Nick had parked. The Jeep started right up with only a few groans. Nick drove his father back to Stephens and the ladies there made such a fuss over him, you'd think he'd been gone for years rather than just a day.

"Nick, I meant to tell you the contractors called and said the beach house would be done next week. It will be good to get back home. See you tomorrow for some chess?"

"Sure, Pop." Nick headed towards the apartment at the beach and could not help but look around him.

I miss this place when I am away, with the constant warm weather, the green trees and flowers everywhere. Yeah, this is home now. This was his life, this was home. Baltimore would always have a special place in his heart but this was home. At least until he returned back to work for the FBI, then his home would be anywhere in the world. He would tell his father of his decision in a couple of days.

He parked along the beach wall and got out to walk in the sand, filling his hands with the pure fine granules and his lungs with the regenerating ocean air. Driving home he turned up the radio to listen to some music, a familiar song was playing on the radio. It was Diesel singing, *I'm Always Coming Home.* How appropriate he thought, and he began to hum along with her sweet melodic voice.

Nick, still humming, pulled into his parking spot at the back of the restaurant and headed for the stairs. Halfway up the stairs he saw Rosa.

"Hi stranger," she said quietly looking lost for words, and lovelier than ever.

"Hi, Rosa," Nick said almost sheepishly. "How are you?" He felt guilty all of a sudden, thinking of Adriana and her memory and what they shared, even for the short time he knew her. It was as if he was denying her and what they had shared. He knew he still had some sorting out to do.

"Better now. I'm so glad you're back. I heard you've been through a lot. Are you back to stay?"

"Yeah. I'm home for awhile."

"Maybe we can get together?"

"I would like that. Give me a day or so to catch up, restock my fridge, do some laundry and then let's do dinner and I will fill you in on everything. How's that?"

"Sounds great, Nick. I heard bits and pieces of some of the stuff you've been through."

"Really?"

"Yeah, I'm with DEA, remember? The Feds know everything."

"Right. How about Saturday night at seven? And this time, dinner is on me. I'll cook."

Nick spent the next couple of days getting his life back in order. It took him a day just to clean up his apartment, go through his mail and go food shopping.

Nick was glad to be home and looking forward to his dinner with Rosa. He shopped all day and even had time to pick up some fresh flowers along the way. Ladies were nuts about flowers. At least his Katie had been crazy about them. Daisies, white daisies, yellow daisies, any kind of daisies, Katie had loved them. But Rosa seemed more like a tulip kind of woman. Red ones.

Nick looked over the apartment and was pleased with his efforts. It looked like a human being lived there and not a bachelor. Again he noticed Katie's picture on the counter—next to it the taunting names of Jess and Linda with the unknown phone number written on the yellow piece of paper. The doorbell rang.

"Hi," said a cheery Rosa, lifting a bottle of wine for Nick's approval while giving him a warm peck on the cheek.

"Molly Dooker, my favorite. How did you know?"

"I asked the owner of Café Luna and he told me you always ordered it when you came into the restaurant."

"Great choice, I'll open the wine and you can choose some nice dinner music for us," he said with a heartfelt smile. He was really glad to see her again but he still missed Adriana. It had been a whirlwind time while he was away and he really did need to decompress. Rosa's calm and steady demeanor would help do just that for him.

"I like your music selection but for dinner, if you don't mind, I am really a very traditional kind of gal."

"Fine, whatever you like."

"What are we having for dinner?"

"I have made a baby green, arugula salad, followed by garlic smashed potatoes mixed with basil and olive oil. For the entrée we are going to have braised lamb shanks with Orzo and asparagus Florentine accompanied by homemade sour cream cornbread scones."

"You are going to spoil me aren't you, Nick?"

"Ah, there's more. For desert, the piece de resistance, we are going to have chocolate lava cake, topped with homemade coconut ice-cream with some Grappa. I've been taking gourmet cooking classes since I've been on leave. It keeps me busy and sane."

"You are hitting all the right buttons tonight, Nick." The music of the soundtrack from *A Man and A Woman* drifted through the apartment as Nick handed her a glass wine.

"Cheers," he said. "To starting over, fresh."

"Cheers, I'll drink to that."

"Ohh, nothing sexier than a man in the kitchen, I like your style. But seriously, I'm glad you're home and in one piece." She walked around his apartment.

"I like your choice of music. Katie and I had seen the movie many times," he said as he sipped his wine.

"Sorry, I did not mean to drag up any bad memories."

"No, this music gives me only good memories."

"Good," she said moving closer, raising her glass, sipping her wine. Her nose brushed his and their lips embraced. They kissed again, longer, sweeter. A buzzer went off in the kitchen, causing an unfortunate timing interruption.

"Duty calls," he told her. "Don't go away."

She sipped her wine and walked behind him into the kitchen, with her finger trailing across his broad shoulders, then down his arm. She walked by his small desk and picked up the picture of him and Katie. "Is this a picture of Katie?"

"Yeah. One of my favorite photos of us."

The yellow piece of paper spiraled to the ground in front of her. She retrieved it off the floor and placed it back in the picture frame and continued her walking tour.

"I didn't know you were into geo-caching? It's great isn't it? I have been doing it for years."

"What is geo-caching?"

"You plant or hide something in a tube, box or whatever will fit in the location you select, a prize or a clue somewhere and give out the coordinates and people you contact try to find it using the geographical coordinates you give them. It's a lot of fun isn't it?"

What was she talking about? Why would she have gotten that impression? Nick furrowed his brow. "I have never done it. What do you mean?"

"Was Katie into geo-caching?"

"No, not that I'm aware. Why do you ask?"

"Oh, nothing, I just saw a tricky geo-cache code on the picture frame on your desk, that's all."

Nick froze, stunned. The blood drained out of his face as he slowly turned his tortured face to look at Rosa. *Did she just ask him what he thought she asked?*

"What do you mean?" he asked slowly.

"That yellow sheet of paper there on your picture frame has a geo-cache code on it, that's all. I'll take some more wine if you don't mind. You also have very good taste in wine and dinner smells delicious." She looked at Nick but it was as if she was not even in the room.

Nick walked to his desk and lifted the picture and removed the yellow sheet. "This is a geo-cache code? It looks more like a phone number since it starts 561 which is the area code for this area of Florida."

"Oh, that, yes. Some people use that to try to disguise their geo-codes."

"What is a geo-code or geo-cache?"

"It has been around for a couple of years ever since smart phones and GPS systems came into play," Rosa said, her face brightened. "It is a great game using GPS coordinates. The prize is sometimes another clue or a small prize. It is a lot of fun. Would you like to try it some weekend?"

"You mean this will give me a location. Can you show me on the computer where this location is?" Nick asked, his heart racing.

"Sure," said Rosa, bewildered, as she set her wine glass down on Nick's wooden desk.

Rosa pulled up Geody.com and typed in the numbers, minus the 561. "Now you add in these numbers on the side, translate these names into numbers and you have 33.889737, -117.7992232 and bingo you're done."

A location popped up on the computer screen, Jessamyn West Park, Yorba Linda, California.

"Jess and Linda, I'll be damned," said Nick. "It wasn't a phone number or name of someone Katie knew after all, but rather a park in California." Nick nearly fell over. "How stupid could I be?"

"What's wrong, Nick?" asked Rosa.

"When my wife was murdered the only clue we had was this piece of paper. I tried to track down its meaning for over a year but with no luck. Now I come to find out it is a clue to who her murderer is. He is taunting me to find him. He's in California."

Rosa stood, and held out her hand to him. "Nick, go to California, find him and then come back to me. I'll be here." She kissed him on the cheek, then embraced him before retrieving her sweater from the sofa and softly closed the door behind her.

Nick was out the door and on his way to the airport within fifteen minutes. He felt terrible about leaving Rosa this evening but he had to go. He'd been trying to solve the mystery of that clue since his Katie was murdered. He would make it up to her somehow, but right now he had to focus.

There were no flights out to California after six p.m. but there was a flight out to Chicago where he could catch a shuteye out later into LAX. It was a nearly three a.m. when he arrived at Los Angeles Airport, dead tired but not to be deterred from his quest.

Nick waited for an hour for the rental car office to open and then the only car they had was one just barely large enough for him to squeeze into. Finally he headed East on I-105.

He headed towards the location of the geo-cache code. There was no other traffic at four in the morning as he turned off onto Route 91. He was getting closer. Nick drove until he almost passed the exit for the Richard Nixon Freeway and headed North.

It took him a total of an hour to find his way until he slowly pulled into the darkened, deserted parking lot at 5 a.m.

Nick followed Rosa's directions from the geo-code exactly and it lead him to the entrance sign proclaiming Jessamyn West Park. He got out of the car, the sounds of traffic with the occasional car speeding by behind him. Crickets chirped incessantly and night bird calls filled the quiet air and thought, what now?

He had come all this way and right now he had no idea what he was looking for. He could hardly see anything since it was still pitch black. Nick noticed two signs, one a welcome sign and another sign which listed the hours the park was open. He could barely see the open ball field and soccer fields beyond the signs.

He remembered what Rosa said in her experience with geo-caching. "You have to look for something that was different or unusual, especially with a cagy geo-cacher." That was so true tonight. He could not see anything in this light. He ran back to the car and put on his headlights to illuminate the two signs.

He looked at both. Nothing was different. They each had a light shining on them with an electrical box underneath, the lights must be on a timer and they were now off. But Nick did a double take. The sign with the hours had two boxes not one.

A pair of eyes watched his every move from the nearby darkness.

Nick knelt down next to the smaller sign and heard a noise in the bushes behind him. He turned, his heart pulsing out of control. He reached for his absent service revolver and just behind him, in the darkness was a deer standing, watching him before lowering his head looking for more grass to chew on.

Nick took a deep breath, hoping that the box was not booby-trapped with a bomb or that he would not be electrocuted. He carefully felt the first box and it had an electrical cable coming from the rear but the second one did not.

Nick reached under the lid, hoping it was not going to explode and pulled. Nothing. Then he pulled again and the lid came free. He reached inside the metal box and pulled out a small metal tin wrapped in plastic.

Nick returned to his small rental car and turned on the flickering dome light, took off the plastic, and found a note inside written on the same yellow paper and the same handwriting as the first one. Careful to grab the edge of the note so as not to destroy any potential DNA or evidence. The note read:

> *Hi Nick-*
> *Glad you stuck with it. You solved the first clue now for your last one.*
> *It's tangy taste makes things sweet*
> *It's dry to be named for water so complete*
> *Tall or short, young or old*
> *Follow this clue if you are bold*
> *Red, white and blue are all around*
> *Time is short, turning color from blue to Wright brown*
> *See you soon Nick before this clue turns you down…*
> *Sorry I could not help you more. Ciao*

Nick had no idea what the clue meant. Where was this new clue going to take him? Was this clue leading him to somewhere else in LA? Nick sat in the car and reread the note. What did it mean? His guys at the agency would be a great start to help him solve this new puzzle. Maybe Dad or Tripp or even Rosa could help him with the new clue.

The trail to find Katie's killer was heating up, having been cold for him for so long. He was back on the trail of Katie's killer. His mind raced with thoughts of finding out what this clue meant.

It was time to turn around and head back home to the East Coast. This clue had nothing to do at all with the West coast—it was directing him home to Florida or Baltimore, was his best guess. All he knew is he didn't want to waste one minute more than he had to track down the killer.

His tiny rental car rolled and bumped along the Los Angeles highway to strands of Bill Withers - *Ain't No Sunshine When She's Gone,* ringing through the radio from an LA oldies station.

Driving to LAX, he thought life was looking up for him and finally he was getting some breaks. Nick would call Tripp as soon as he got home. He had a new clue, a new lead. Yeah, life was looking up.

By dawn and Nick was just starting to doze in one of the airport's tall comfortable leather massage chairs. His flight did not leave for another two hours. It had been a long day, if he could only close his eyes, just for a moment and sleep, he would feel so much better. His cell phone rang and his caller ID told him it was Rosa.

"Hi," she said. "I thought maybe you could use the sound of a familiar voice."

"Yeah, it is real good to hear from you. I can't tell you how good. Sorry about last night. I found a new clue, and she had him read it twice to her.

Rosa was quiet at first but then, "I have some thoughts," she said at last. "We can kick them around if you like when you get home. It is as strange as the first clue."

"I am heading back to Florida but I am stopping in Baltimore first for a day, sorry."

"Why Baltimore?"

"I am going to deliver this latest note to the FBI Forensic Lab Headquarters and see if they can tell me anything about it. Maybe it has some DNA, or they can analyze the handwriting or even the paper. Then I'll see where that takes me."

"Tell you what, when you get back to Florida I'll take off work for a day or so." chimed in Rosa. "Then come over to my place and we will talk about this latest clue and see what we can figure out."

"Sounds great. I appreciate all of your help. If it wasn't for you I would never have this new clue. I don't know how to thank you."

"I'll think of something. We can pick up where we left off. I'll reheat the dinner, we'll open another bottle of wine, and we can talk and then let you get lost in my arms. Or maybe if you're lucky, we'll just skip the dinner entirely. How does that sound?"

"Yeah, sounds great. I'll call you when I get in. Thanks for being so understanding. See you when I get back."

Nick smiled, thinking of Rosa and hummed himself to sleep, the now familiar Diesel tune, *I'm Always Comin' Home...*"

Now he was headed back to Baltimore, again. Every time he tried to leave, he kept getting drawn back there.

Chapter Forty-One

Nick was awakened in his large comfortable chair by the announcement over the loudspeaker calling all passengers to begin boarding his flight. Once onboard he grabbed a pillow from the overhead and pulled the note from his pocket again. He read it so much he almost had it memorized.

Hi Nick-
Glad you stuck with it. You solved the first clue now for your last one.
It's tangy taste makes things sweet
It's dry to be named for water so complete
Tall or short, young or old
Follow this clue if you are bold
Red, white and blue are all around
Time is short, turning color from blue to Wright brown
See you soon Nick before this clue turns you down…
Sorry I could not help you more. Ciao

He hoped the longer he looked at it the more sense it would make. What the hell did it mean?

The flight to Baltimore was pretty uneventful but the bumpy landing jolted him back to reality. He threw his carryon bag over his shoulder and made his way towards the carousel.

Nick decided he desperately needed a shower, a change of clothes and some rest. He would take a taxi home and sleep there for a few hours and see if he could get Katie's car started. He could use her car for the short while he was in Baltimore. It would bring back memories.

While waiting for his luggage to arrive, he noticed the grey haired lady who had sat beside him on the plane, walking with her family to retrieve their bags. He managed a small smile as she stopped beside him, two kids in tow. He took a deep breath.

"Hi there, don't they look just like their pictures?" she said, pointing to the two kids, she'd talking about on the ride. "See what I mean. This one is Daniel and this pretty lady is my Rachel. Say hello children."

He heard mumbled greetings from the kids, while they searched for something more interesting to occupy them. The older one, Rachel, was checking her cell phone for text messages.

"Grandma, how much longer are we going to be here? My friends want me to meet them at the mall."

"Well when we get finished here, your father would like to take all of us out for steamed crabs. Isn't that grand?"

"Ugh, but grandma, crabs are so messy and spicy. Yuck!"

"The meat is so sweet because the Old Bay Seasoning flavors it right up," said the now defensive Grandma. She could have promised to take them anywhere in the world, and would have brought on similar protests.

Nick grabbed his suitcase from the baggage claim and headed for the taxi stand. A waiting taxi sped away from the stand and soon he was on his way home. He had the taxi driver stop at a seven-eleven on the way and he picked up some coffee, milk and a few other staples to hold him over. He had plenty of canned goods still in his pantry but no coffee. He needed his morning coffee.

He soon found himself standing in front of his old stone manor house by the stream. He was glad now that he didn't sell it. It was his refuge and better than staying in a downtown motel.

Nick's father was always pestering him to put down roots one place or another and he had come close to selling it but there was plenty of time for that. He just wasn't ready yet. He sent Rosa a text telling her he'd arrived and that he would talk to her soon.

He could still make out the blood stains on the stone floor in the living of the old house where Jenkins and Gaskins had died. He did not have the energy to do anything about it right now. Tomorrow was another day. He slid into his old bed, the bed he had shared with Katie, and immediately drifted off to sleep.

He thought as he drifted off to sleep about the grandma, her grandkids and the note. The kid was right they were messy but the Old Bay seasoning made the tough crabs sweet. Wait—sweet! Old Bay!

He shot straight up in bed and turned on the light, rushing to find his pants, reaching for the note from his pocket.

Its tangy taste makes things sweet
It's dry to be named for water so complete

Old Bay seasoning, named after the Maryland Chesapeake Bay and Maryland crabs. He was on the right trail. Old Bay named after the Chesapeake Bay made the crab meat taste so sweet.

Red, white and blue are all around.

Fort McHenry and the huge flag that flew there, yes he was definitely on the right track. The note had led him back to Baltimore but what did the rest of the clue mean?

Chapter Forty-Two

"Hey Tripp, this is Nick. I need your help. I have another note about Katie's death. I am going to drop it off at the Forensics Lab in Baltimore. Give me a call when you get this message." Nick closed his cell phone after leaving the voicemail.

He knew the clue led him here to Baltimore but Baltimore was a big city. Where should he start looking for the killer? And was this the end of the chase or would it lead him only to another clue, then another? At this point Nick had more clues than answers. He didn't care how many clues he had to track down, he would find Katie's killer.

Nick still had another portion of the clue that he could try to decipher as he headed down to the basement garage of the house. The sight of Katie's car stopped him dead in his tracks. He could not breathe, he could not move, just from the sight of it.

Nick removed the old nylon cover from the old silver Porsche and Nick soon had the battery reconnected. He opened up the garage door to let in some air. The 356B Porsche Speedster started right up, but coughed, as it ingested the old gasoline, water and related muck at the bottom of its gas tank. The car sputtered and died, leaving just a blast of blue smoke lingering in the air. He restarted the old car again and it finally roared to a renewed life, soon humming a sweet tune to the music of the flathead six-cylinder.

He checked to make sure his tags had not expired. The last thing he needed was a ticket for expired tags. He had two months left on them.

The car savored the curving, twisty country roads and the low slung German masterpiece clung to the ground. He had forgotten how much he loved driving this car, holding the steering wheel in his hands was like holding Katie. He embraced the car as the car hugged the road.

The guard at the FBI Registration desk asked for an ID before giving him a visitors badge to visit the forensics lab as the mangaer signed him into the secure FBI building.

"Hello Agent Ryan. I am Stanton Deterges, Forensics Lab Manager. Assistant Director Jackson called and said to give you any assistance you may require. What can I do for you, sir?" asked the tall thin man, wearing an oversized white lab coat, with dark hair and small dark framed glasses, which were much too small for his face.

"Do you mean, Tripp?"

"Yes, sir."

Nick shrugged and showed him the letter still in the plastic wrapped bag.

"Follow me sir." He turned and headed down the long white tiled corridor. At the end of the hallway he placed his chin on a resting pad while it performed a retinal scan and then inserted his fingers into a fingerprint scanner to gain access. A loud click echoed in the air and the door swung open, leading into a large forensics lab with offices along the whole perimeter of the large room.

Deterge marched to a large sterile table and laid the items Nick had given him onto a sterile tray. He put on a pair of green sterile gloves as Nick winced, thinking of the cavalier way he had mistakenly handled this important forensic evidence.

"I did try to be careful when handling the document but there may be some of my DNA on it," Nick said while peering over the man's shoulder.

The lab manager turned and peered over his shoulder looking down over his glasses, saying, "I'm sure you did, sir." He started to say something else, but must have thought better of it. "Yes sir, I am sure you did," he repeated before turning back to the evidence in front of him.

Ryan leaned over his shoulder to get a closer look at the note before the Technician turned to him and said, "Agent Ryan, have you had lunch yet?"

"No. I am not really hungry or interested in eating. I am more interested in this note."

"I suggest lunch, Agent Ryan."

"Well, okay. Would you like to join me?"

"No, sir. May I suggest you go to lunch and let us thoroughly examine this evidence? I can then call you with any results we may have."

"That is a crucial piece of evidence in a murder case I am working on Mr. Deterge and I am very reluctant to let it out of my sight. I am sure that you can appreciate that, can you not?"

The short, balding lab manager took off his glasses and turned to face Ryan. "Agent Ryan I am sure that you are very good at what you do. Director Jackson spoke very highly of you. But we are the best chance of helping you solve your wife's murder, if you will let us do our job. We are very good, if not the best in the world, at what we do. Go have some lunch. Okay, Agent Ryan?"

Ryan reluctantly agreed. He had the lab manager make a copy of the letter to take with him. Stanton protested at first about messing with evidence, but soon saw it was futile to disagree with Special Agent Ryan.

Fifteen minutes later Nick hopped back into the Porsche and began driving around aimlessly. He soon found himself on Charles Street, a wide tree lined road which ran through some of the oldest neighborhoods and the largest mansions in the city. He checked his cell phone at a traffic light to make sure it was on and noticed he had a message waiting for him from Tripp.

"Nick, old buddy. I got your message. I am back in Pakistan but I called the Lab in Baltimore and asked them to help you in any way they could." Nick smiled when he heard the message. He knew he could always count on Tripp.

The Teutonic Porsche made its way through the city, driving aimlessly, with no particular place to go until Nick found himself in front of the campus where Katie used to work, TAPL. He looked down the broad avenue leading to the main building and turned slowly down his own memory lane.

He passed the various buildings named after many large donors. Nick pulled into the nearby employee parking lot, with Katie's blue parking permit visibly displayed, and parked the old Porsche.

Nick walked around the office campus. It was designed to feel more like a school or University than the highly secret research lab that it truly was. He walked into the Quadrangle and saw the windows of Katie's old office straight ahead of him. Nick was drawn like a magnet ever closer to the tree shrouded space, the place where she had worked, had lunch on sunny days and would meet him before they would go out for their dates. The memories came flooding back to him.

In the center of the square was a huge sculpture depicting the life cycle of the Maryland Blue Crab donated by Ralph Herdsman. He was a local billionaire who showered money onto the facilities at various times over the years.

Nick stopped and looked past the large metal sculpture to see Katie's office window. She hated the metal monstrosity even though she had to look at it every day. It had destroyed the wonderful view of the Quadrangle she had before it was erected.

The crab sculpture portrayed the transition in life from the Zoeae, to Megalops, to the small Juveniles to the Adult crab. While Katie liked the metal storytelling, she did not like the last part, which showed the crab coming out of the steamer pot covered with Old Bay Seasoning, ready to be devoured by the faithful.

Nick noticed the steamed crab held his claws defiantly high in the air, pincers pointed at each other. Nick could see in the background behind the claw had two windows centered on it, one was Katie's and the other a former co worker, Natalie Wortman. Katie always thought that Natalie had a thing for Nick, because of the way she acted when Nick was around. Nick only had eyes for his Katie and she knew it.

He saw the Katie's office window positioned between the claws. Something was causing his mental engine to rev up. Nick looked at the dedication plaque on the front of the crabs and saw the name of the sculptor, Mr. Wright Brown. In his latest clue, the message ended in;

Time is short, turning color from blue to Wright brown

When the Maryland blue crab was steamed it turned from blue to red and the sculpture was done by Wright Brown.

He was in the right place, he knew it, he could feel it. He noticed also the small campus clock was directly under Natalie's office. Time was short. But what next? His cell phone rang, jarring his concentration. It was the lab.

"Agent Ryan? This is Stanton Deterges, FBI Forensics Lab Manager."

"Yes. Hi. What did you find out?"

"Well, we are still testing the document you gave us but so far we have determined that the note was written by the same person who wrote the first note because the handwriting matches exactly. The person who wrote it is right handed and English is not their native language. The paper used is also the same, and appears to have come from a small note pad, easily available anywhere." Stanton paused and Nick could tell from the tone of his voice he was quite pleased with himself.

"Good information, Stanton. Anything else?"

"Yes, Agent Ryan. This letter, while it sounds to be a source of mockery and poetry, was written quickly and under extreme distress. Much like you would see a note written scribbled in haste before getting on a plane, waiting for a cab or something like that. I feel this note was not written by the murderer but by someone who is trying to help you in the general direction of further discovery without giving away their own identity."

"Good job, Stanton. I will mention your quick work to Director Jackson the next time I speak with him."

"Thank you, sir. If we discover anything else, we will be back in touch."

Nick put his cell phone away and looked again at the huge crab towering over him. Where to next? He thought about his next move and he turned to walk away, and came face to face with Natalie Wortman.

"Hi ya, Nick," she said with the sweetest smile, tilting her head to one side so seductively.

Chapter Forty-Three

Massac Arum buttoned his white collared shirt and tied his tie, pulling it snug up against his neck. He put on his dress oxfords and slipped on his suit coat.

When Massac finished dressing, he looked at himself in the full length mirror hanging on the back of the closet door. The top hinges of the door were loose and the door hung at an angle, looking like at any moment it would fall off its frame.

"Morning, Mr. President," he said to himself, holding his microphone directly in the president's face while looking in the mirror.

"Morning Mr. Arum," he replied to himself, touching the top of his forehead in a mock salute. He placed the special microphone into his briefcase. He was ready.

Massac walked down the back stairs of his old apartment building on the south side of District Heights, in the poorest immigrant section of Washington, D.C. The area reminded him of the other slums he had lived in Iraq and Somalia, only the streets were cleaner but just as dangerous.

He started up the old Ford sedan and headed for the convention center. He had to be there early otherwise he would lose his job and not even the union could help him this time. He had asked for the day off which guaranteed he would be assigned to work today. His boss had it in for him. He needed this job.

The young immigrant from the Middle East had spent time with the Marines fighting side by side with them in Iraq and Somali. They fought together and shed blood together but American beliefs were not his beliefs. He watched and learned their ways.

Now he was in the America and had been given a reporters job at a local TV station before being hired as a stringer for one of the networks. His new job gave him unlimited access to sensitive locations. He had come to America, the land of opportunity and he was going to make the most of it.

Massac knew his job and he was very good at it, even one of his roommates Iatr, told him he was good. He joined the ever growing White House press corps for the new President, John Alexander. He liked the prior President better than Alexander because he felt he was looking out for all foreign guests. This new one seemed detached and disinterested.

"God, you're here early for once, Arum," said the DC security Sergeant, Larry Height. "The OPP and the Secret Service are sweeping the upper sections now. The lower section and the entrance have already been done. You can join the other reporters in the press briefing room, just over there. President Alexander will be entering through that door," he said handing him his security badge.

"Yes, Sarge. Whatever you say. I'll get right over there. I thought the OPP was going to be disbanded?"

"Just do your job and don't ask any questions, okay?"

"But Sarge, I'm a reporter, my job is asking questions." He joined the others from the various news organizations who normally followed the President and made idle chit chat while he glanced at his watch. It would be another three hours before the new President would show up. May as well make himself comfortable.

Chapter Forty-Four

"I saw Katie's car on the employee lot and figured it was probably you," Natalie said, as she continued to smile. "Did you come to visit or reminisce?" She smiled a much too friendly smile for Nick. It was a smile that always made him feel a little uncomfortable. He could not explain why, it just did.

She stood there, tall, nearly as tall as Nick, with dark brown hair and twinkling emerald green eyes and wearing a snug navy blue outfit. Her hair was pulled back revealing a small butterfly tattoo just under her right earlobe.

Katie had liked Natalie at first. They would spend time together every day at work having lunch, shopping and Natalie was a constant guest at the Ryan house for dinner. That friendship stopped when Katie got promoted to a special department inside TAPL. Natalie seemed to take offense that she was not the one promoted instead.

After her promotion, Katie found Natalie constantly badgering her for information about her new job. Katie could not share anything about The Lab with anyone, including Nick. But Katie also thought that Natalie flirted with Nick whenever the opportunity arose.

"I've missed you, Nick," she said, turning away from the crab sculpture behind them. "Very interesting piece isn't it? Did you happen to notice who did the work? It was done by Wright Brown. He is very famous in his own right."

"Yes, he is."

"Nick can we go somewhere? I need to talk to you. I think you are in danger if you stay here. Can we go, now?" Before Nick could answer a booming voice enveloped both of them, it was the unmistakable voice of Dr. Richard Rome, Katie's former boss and Natalie's boyfriend.

"Well, look who it is? If it isn't old Nick Ryan, Special Agent for the FBI. How the hell are you, Nick?" The good doctor gave Natalie a peck on the cheek and put his arm around her waist, holding her close to him.

"Good to see you again, Dr. Rome."

Richard Rome was British and from the old school. With his wavy grey hair, pencil thin black and grey mustache and his ever present Donegal tweed jacket and perfectly tied bowtie, he reeked of the British Empire.

Katie and Nick had been to his house many times for dinner while his wife and he were still married. Richard had told everyone his wife Malory went back to Sweden to stay with her ailing mother but she never returned. He was a changed man after that, not being his usual sociable self but today he sounded like the old Richard.

"What brings you back to our beautiful town and to our humble workplace?"

"Well this is far from humble digs here, Doc. I am still investigating Katie's murder and thought I might be able to turn up some leads here since she spent so much time at work."

"Still looking for her killer, huh?"

"Yeah, I'll never stop looking."

"I guess the well is pretty dried up as far as leads go, wouldn't you say, Nick? You just didn't have any luck. You know how that goes," said the smug Dr. Rome.

Nick's back stiffened with anger. Rome had been of very little help the last time he was here, looking for leads and seemed to care even less now about Katie's killer.

"Well, to be truthful with you, the reason I am here is I just uncovered another note which gives me more clues about Katie's murder. So I thought I would snoop around some more. It seemed to be directing me here. Natalie and I were just discussing it."

"Is that so, Nick?" The scholarly Physicist pulled Natalie even closer. "Well, why don't the three of us have some lunch and we can talk about it. You know what they say, three heads are better than one. We may be able to provide you some input because we live in this place nearly all of the time. Perhaps we can help?"

Natalie shot him a telling glance, which Nick did not know how to read.

Nick always sensed that there was a rivalry between Dr. Rome and everybody else at the Top Secret research campus. Katie told him many times of the things he would do and say to try to find out what other departments were working on. He was a likeable sort but ever since his divorce he became even more distant than before.

"Well okay, sure," said Nick. *Everybody wants me to go have lunch. Do I look hungry or something?*

"I'm parked right over here in the staff lot," said Richard. "We can go to my house, it is just a short way off campus."

Nick saw the big black Mercedes parked in front of the sign announcing, Reserved—Dr. Rome as he slid into the back seat. The car still had the mixed scent of leather, wood and plastic permeating the interior.

"Nothing like it, that new car smell," said Nick.

"Yes, indeed," said Rome backing up and pulling onto Charles Street, heading North. "Tell me about the note you found, Nick. Where did you find it?"

Nick considered if he would tell Dr. Rome all he knew. He really shouldn't tell investigation secrets, but if he were going to get some more information, then perhaps what he found would spark something in Katie's old friends' minds. "I found it a small park outside of Los Angeles."

"Is that so?" Rome took a sudden interest in the note, his eyebrows raised. The man shot a glance at Natalie.

"Yes it was a small little league park called Jessamyn West Park, in Yorba Linda."

"Interesting Nick, very interesting. And that note, it sent you here?"

"Yes, I think so. It was more like a riddle but as I solved one portion of the riddle it made the rest easier. But I am still working on it."

Rome drove the full-sized Mercedes into the driveway entrance of one the largest old, white brick and marble mansions which populated the area. The front shutters were painted a traditional British racing green color. A small model of a red-jacketed jockey, holding a gas lamp greeted them as they drove by the front of the house and around the rear.

Tall trees lined the rear yard, overhanging and touching at the top, providing shade and welcome relief from the hot sun.

Very stately, thought Nick, exiting the car and following the others up the driveway towards the house. They walked up the rear steps of the old wooden porch which overlooked a beautifully manicured lawn and garden. *Very nice but how can he afford all of this? The university must have him on a high salary.*

Nick knew Rome's wife Malory came from money, big money from Sweden, but now that they were divorced, that had to have dried up by now.

"Let me show you around," said a suddenly friendly Rome. "I'll give you the five-cent tour." He led them through the downstairs, pointing out the valuable art work, the expensive Persian rugs and the fine china in the nearby cabinet before leading them upstairs to his dark walnut paneled den. The whole place reeked of money, old money, thought Nick.

Rome sat behind the desk and said, "Could I see the note, Nick?"

"Yes," said Nick, "if you think you can help." He pulled a copy of the note from his pocket and handed it to him. "Nice place, Doc."

"Thank you, Nick," he said, without looking up from examining the note laid out before him on his huge desk.

"Interesting and very interesting handwriting. You are a complicated fellow, Nick. I always admired that about you. You are a bulldog and you never let go of something until you got your man. Tell me Nick, this note led you here, to Baltimore and our lab?"

"Yes, indeed. But like I said, I still am figuring out the rest of it. I'll figure it out, sooner or later."

"Hmm. Nick, what do you make of the last word in the note, *Ciao*?"

"Well it is Italian," Nick started. "They use it to say hello and goodbye. It is also a term of affection, like *Ciao Bella*, goodbye beautiful."

"Well the Italians mainly use the word that way," Rome said, "but when you are in the capital of Italy they say it for both hello and goodbye."

"Well that would be, Rome," interjected Nick.

Natalie made a choking sound beside Nick.

"Yes, that is correct Nick." Rome looked straight at him.

Nick finally connected the dots. It was Rome—Dr. Rome! Nick reacted immediately, darting from his chair. "You?" he shouted, pointing at Rome he lunged at the man.

Rome pulled a black semi-automatic Glock handgun from his desk drawer, "Hold it right there, Nick, my boy. Sit down." He trained the gun on Nick.

"I knew it was only a matter of time before you put all the pieces together. I just sped up the process. We are going for a little ride and you won't be coming back I'm afraid."

"You? Why did you have to kill my, Katie? Why? What did she ever do to you?"

Rome leveled the gun at Nick's chest. "When my wife divorced me all the money stopped but not the bills. The bills kept coming. Then I only had my paycheck to support this life I had grown so accustomed to living."

Natalie sobbed uncontrollably as he continued. "I needed more money desperately and the Russians, Iranians and Chinese were more than willing to pay vast amounts of money for some of the secrets we have developed here at the labs. They pay very well. There came a time when they wanted more and were willing to pay a lot of money for it." He shifted the gun from one hand to the other, still keeping it pointed directly at Nick.

"The secrets they wanted were only available in the Lab that Katie controlled. I knew she would never go along with it so I had to kill her.

Rome cleared his throat, clearly enjoying having the upper hand. "In order to get into a secure lab I needed her fingerprints to get through the fingerprint access equipment at the lab. That's why I cut off her hands. I hated to do it, but it was either her or me. Sorry, Nick."

He tossed Natalie the Mercedes keys saying, "You drive."

Nick seethed with anger, his hands turning white while he gripped the armchair. "Did you know about this Natalie?".

"I found out by accident only after he killed her," she said. "He told me he would kill me too if I told anyone," Natalie sobbed. "That is why I had to be careful about leaving the notes for you, so he did not know they came from me. I was only trying to help. I'm sorry Nick there was nothing else I could do. You know I loved Katie."

"Shut up, Natalie. I'll take care of you later. Stand up Nick, and don't try anything funny."

"How will you explain this?" Nick asked.

"Don't worry, a distraught husband, a former lover and a gun can produce some pretty telling evidence."

"We were never lovers," cried Natalie.

"I know that, but the cops won't know that. Now move."

They walked towards the steps and Natalie suddenly made a move for the gun, grabbing Rome's hand. Nick was on him in a flash, trying to wrestle the gun from him.

The pistol roared in a flash of thunder and smoke, the bullet struck Natalie in the chest, causing her to crumple to the floor. Blood spewed from her chest, as the surprise look on her face registered the shock of what happened. She collapsed onto the soft cream carpet below.

Nick shoved Rome and tried to tackle him, entangling his arms and hands, relying on his Marine and FBI training. But Rome was tough, having spent years in the British Grenadiers.

Rome and Nick struggled. "Give it up, Doc, you'll never get away with it."

Nick had him in an arm lock and then gave him a hard rabbit punch to his ribs.

Rome's hands went high in the air as he slipped and fell backwards, head over feet, tumbling down the long steep marble stairway. He landed with a loud thud at the bottom. He wasn't moving.

Nick held Natalie as he knelt down next to her, he could tell she was going fast."Hold on. I'm going to call 911 and get you some help!"

"No Nick. It's too late. I am so sorry, Nick. I am so sorry," was all she could manage and then she was gone. Nick lowered her to the floor and went to check on Rome. His neck was broken and his face was contorted in a death mask.

Natalie was dead. Katie was dead, all so that Rome could live in style in a big old mansion.

Nick picked up the phone in the hallway and dialed 911. "Hello 911, there's been an accident. I want to report an accidental death."

Nick was questioned by the police for the next four hours, laying the whole story out for them, until they finally released him. He picked up Katie's Porsche and headed home. But first he had a stop to make along the way.

It was almost closing time, as the silver two-seater pulled into Saint Stanislaus Cemetery on Dundalk Avenue in a quiet residential neighborhood. Nick had picked up some daisies at the flower stand out in front of the entrance gate and made his way down the third aisle amid a sea of burial markers. He stopped at the white headstone which bore the name Katherine Ryan.

He caressed the smooth top of the grave marker with his hand. "Hi ya' doing, my love? It's me, Nicky. I miss you like crazy."

He placed the flowers gently on her grave and knelt down to whisper in her ear. "I won't be seeing you for awhile, my sweet. You are going to have to just wait for me. I don't know how long but we will have our eternity together. I love you more than ever, but I think I now understand some things better." He kissed the stone and caressed the smooth marble on the top.

"Goodbye, Katie. I love you. I'll always love you."

Chapter Forty-Five

The President's motorcade wound its way through the nation's capital on its way to the convention center. President Alexander was due to make a major announcement about the expansion of his predecessor's teacher program. He was also going to announce some major new arms development programs that would be sure to set off a new expensive arms race with the rest of the world.

The big limo pulled up to the entrance, amid the flash of cameras and TV crews. "Good afternoon, everyone," President Alexander said with a huge political smile. "I am glad that you could all attend today. We have a lot to talk about."

He shook hands and talked to reporters, smiling while he made his way into the awaiting auditorium. He loved this and it showed. He was right where he was supposed to be and he was going to make the most of it. *Now was the beginning,* he thought to himself, *the beginning of the end.*

He saw Massac Arum, the reporter with one of the networks waving him over, "Mr. President, ITN Network News, sir. If you have a moment, please sir. I just have one question, please."

Reluctantly the President trudged to the awaiting reporter, and his upheld microphone. He remembered that Arum's questions always seemed to come out of left field. But he reasoned that if he continued, he would just have Arum's White House credentials pulled and that would be the end of it.

"Good day, Mr. Arum," he said while still shaking hands being thrust at him from all sides.

"Mr. President, is it true that you hated the former President, Careb Hussein because of his religious beliefs? Can you confirm or deny that, Mr. President?" he challenged, sticking the microphone directly in front of the President's face.

Alexander was stunned at the question but was distracted by the strange hole at the end of the microphone.

Suddenly Arum began yelling, "Death to all non-believers, death to the infidels!" and pulled the trigger of the homemade device. The bullet found its target, penetrating the President's head. He was dead before he hit the ground.

Secret Service agents swarmed all over Massac Arum and wrestled him to the floor. The ambulance, which always accompanied the President to every meeting, rushed the President away to the hospital. He was pronounced dead upon arrival. America had lost two Presidents in the space of one week. It would have a new President by dawn. America was in mourning over its second loss of leadership coming so soon after the death of James Galloway. The rest of the world lost another *Kitman* without even knowing about it.

Chapter Forty-Six

"Goodbye, old house," Nick said to his place by the stream, as he finished packing the little speedster for his drive to Florida.

"I will miss you and all of the sweet memories that you hold dear to me and to Katie." All of the memories came rushing back to him. As he got into his car, passing the For Sale sign, he thought, about those sweet memories, but it was time to say good bye, to start a new life.

It took Nick three days to drive to Delray with stops along the way. He jumped off of I-95 as he reached Palm Beach County. The ride down A1A was relaxing and the drive from Baltimore had given him a lot of time to clear his head and think about his future. He decided he was staying put in Florida and he was not going back to the FBI.

Nick could live off the money he had in the bank from the life insurance settlement on Katie and to keep busy he could take the occasional insurance investigating work that came his way. He could also spend some more time with his father. And then there was Rosa. Maybe now they could have the dinner they'd been trying to have for weeks.

Nick pulled into the rear of Luna Rosa and parked his car. Grabbing the two boxes and an over the shoulder bag he made his way up the back steps. He stopped at the top of the landing and scoured the parking lot, looking for Rosa's car. No luck. Just as well. *I can use a shower, shave and a change of clothes before I see her.* He showered, shaved and chilled some wine in the fridge. After one last check in the mirror and he headed next door. He was about to knock on Rosa's door, when a portly man with a marinara splattered white shirt interrupted him.

"Hi ya, Nick. Welcome back," said Tito, the head chef at Café Luna Rosa and his landlord.

"Hey, Tito. Good to see you. I was looking for Rosa."

"She's not here. She got transferred to Arizona for some hush, hush assignment. She won't be back for a long while. That's all she could tell me. She wanted to call you but you know how the DEA is about letting people discuss things like that."

"Yeah, I understand. If you talk to her, tell her I am back, for good."

"Sure Nick. But she did leave this note for you."

Nick opened the pink envelope and pulled out a piece of notepaper, pink flamingoes adorning the edge.

Nick-
Sorry we could never get together. Rain check???
See you when I get back.
Love,
Rosa

Nick smiled folding the paper and putting it into his pocket.

"Hey Nick, would you like some dinner?" Tito asked.

"I would love to, but I think I am going over to visit with my father."

"So I'll make two to go. Comin' right up. I'm just sorry Rosa isn't here to greet you."

Nick went back to his apartment, pulled out his cell phone and dialed. It rang twice before a familiar voice answered, "Hello?"

"Hey Pop. You want me to bring you some Italian? Maybe we can play some chess? I'll even let you choose, white or black."

"Sure Nicky, sure."

"Okay, pop. I'll see you in fifteen minutes. Love ya, Pop."

Life was returning to normal. Life was good again.

Nick went back to the fridge to grab a six pack of beer for his dad and left, walking past the flashing red light of his answering machine.

He had five new messages waiting for him. They would have to wait until tomorrow. Everything would have to wait; Nick Ryan was home, home to stay.

-The End-

6642624R00126

Made in the USA
San Bernardino, CA
12 December 2013